DRAGON'S KITTY

Dragon Point Nine

EVE LANGLAIS

Dragon Point

Prologue

Before Kitty almost ended the world, she—a female of a mature five years, who'd thank-fully managed to avoid the impregnation trap suffered by her other litter mates—roamed the streets, stealing scraps and hunting rats whilst evading death. Good thing she still had seven lives left, as the streets could be hard and existence often short.

That all changed when she freed a Jinn from a glass bottle—rolled that sucker right off the edge of the shelf where it taunted her. The smoky presence she released initially scared her. In a panic, Kitty wished to be somewhere else and *poof*! She appeared in the middle of a desert, where she encountered a dragon in human form. It should be noted she had little use for the two-legged unless they had food to give.

She couldn't have said what appealed to her about the oversized male atop the boney beast that carried it; however, when he scooped up Kitty and placed her in the most regal of positions—in front of him on his steed—she decided to keep him on as her servant.

Thus far, it had worked in her favor. He fed her from his plate, the best parts of course. Scratched her with the right amount of pressure behind the ears. Stroked her fur until it became sleek. He also led an interesting life that involved much exploration—oftentimes in places with prey for her to hunt.

When they weren't scouring the world for his enemies, they stayed in a lovely home with plenty of holes in the walls for her to investigate, mice to eat, and a chance to show off to other less fortunate felines who envied her majestic nature and devoted, two-legged servant.

A servant deeply troubled.

Her little brain had a hard time grasping why he seemed malcontent. How she wished she could understand.

And suddenly she did. The street cat went from having simple thoughts and desires to being a complex being with insight thanks to the jinn she'd released. Everyone knew jinn—also known as Shaitan and genies depending on the level of power —always gave three wishes. She'd now used two.

The second allowed her to perceive the world in a new fashion that fed her curiosity. A dangerous thing for a feline with several lives left and one last wish.

But first... Where was her servant with her dinner?

Chapter One

The cat in Israfil's lap purred as he stroked its silken fur. He'd never been one for felines, or canines for that matter. The only thing close to a pet that he ever owned was his horse, Kliiv, who'd served him well and continued to do so even after death.

Years spent carefully carving runes in a bone left behind by his steed meant when he returned to the world, he could count on Kliiv's solid presence. Magic gave the soul he'd kept a corporeal form, with a few modifications such as a coat dark as night, eyes blazing red, and height. Kliiv now stood several handspans taller than he had in life, and when Israfil's mount huffed through his nostrils, the smoke held a hint of sulfur, while the hooves left sparks when clipping across rock.

"I really don't see why we came here, Kitty."

Israfil bestowed upon the feline a simple name because she rejected everything else. Kitty had a very distinct way of making her feelings known. Feed her the wrong thing? She'd slice your hand open. Didn't give her petting when demanded? More scratches.

Her demanding nature actually endeared her to him, not that he'd ever admit it. It would ruin his reputation. As to how they came to be a pair...

She'd been in the desert when he'd emerged from a three-thousand-year imprisonment, sitting calmly on her haunches, expression haughty, clearly waiting for him to pick her up. He'd been carting her around ever since. At times, he felt like her servant.

Ridiculous, of course. As if he'd ever serve a cat.

Kitty glanced at him and blinked.

"Don't give me that look. I'm aware of why we came, but I'd still rather be anywhere else. Maybe I'll get lucky and admitting I need help will kill me." A man could hope, even if it hadn't worked in the past.

"Meow." Kitty uncurled herself and leapt from the high back of the horse to the ground.

"I'll whine if I want to," he huffed, slipping off his mount. How far he'd fallen. A dragon mage arguing with his cat. A cat who couldn't even speak!

Used to be, Israfil didn't have to ask for help

because he'd been a knowledgeable person with all the answers. But that was in the old world. Time passed while he essentially stood still. The modern world arrived, and he'd yet to completely catch up. For all he'd learned since his release, there remained much he didn't understand. Technology being a prime example. He still didn't grasp phones and how they allowed people to talk across great distances. And this thing they called television? Why watch a performance on a box rather than in person?

Blame humans. Since they couldn't wield magic, they built. Roads, buildings, vehicles that could fly. The world was a much different place now, and the dragons he used to lord over had changed with it. His kind had gone from being top of the evolutionary chain to hiding from humans. They hid their existence because, apparently, dragons had been almost wiped out. Their own fault for banishing the dragon mages!

He still couldn't believe their arrogant nerve. Even now, the descendants of his people refused to properly bow to the mages who not only beat them in power but age. Their lack of respect would lead to Israfil teaching them a lesson about honoring their betters, but only after he got rid of all the Shaitan.

Nasty creatures from another dimension. They'd caused such havoc in his time. He'd lost many friends and family in the Shaitan wars to the invasive race determined to bring about the end of the world. It might be an improvement, given the blight of humans upon it.

There were so many of them now. What a waste of space. Why couldn't some tasty sheep or delicious goats have been the ones to multiply in the billions?

He returned to the moment and tucked his Kliiv-summoning bone into his pocket as he observed the electrified fence in front of him. It surrounded the compound owned by the Silvergrace family, a Sept of silver dragons who served a golden king. A king who wasn't a mage and who'd married a shifter. Appalling. But he'd not come to discuss their lack of etiquette or politics, but rather—

"The chef is serving pecan pie, if you're hungry."

The sudden feminine voice by his side startled. He'd never heard her approach, and neither had his cat. A discomfited Kitty quickly climbed Israfil to sit on his shoulder. He'd learned to not wince at the pinprick of claws when she did this.

What he couldn't ignore was the woman who'd appeared, heavily pregnant, wearing a yellow frock. How had she suddenly appeared? She wasn't a mage, nor did she wear any invisibility tokens.

"Did the cat actually get your tongue?" she

teased with a grin. "I've seen it happen in a few of your futures. Which reminds me, warning, don't forget to feed Kitty."

At her words, he suddenly placed who this woman was despite their never having met. He left communication with the lesser dragons to Jeebrelle, who appeared to have a fondness for one called Babette. He didn't pay much mind to what the modern Septs did; however, this woman? He'd heard of her. "You are the seer, Elspeth."

"And you're Israfil, mighty horseman of the apocalypse, also known as War." The seer beamed at him. "I've been looking forward to meeting you."

He frowned. "Why?"

It never boded well when a seer showed an interest. Just look at what Maalik had done to the original thirteen dragon mages. Claimed the world would end unless they agreed to be frozen until they were needed again. It didn't sound horrible at the time. The reality proved different than expectation. The frozen part only applied to aging because they lived—and had been tortured—every second of every day as they waited to be spit out upon the world again.

Kitty leaped from his shoulder and paced around the pregnant woman before seating herself at her feet.

"You're going to do wonderful things, you and

your adorable Kitty." Elspeth crouched and reached for the feline.

Kitty tilted her head and allowed the scratch.

Traitor. She was only supposed to purr when he did it. He scowled. "Don't you dare predict my future."

Elspeth glanced at him over her shoulder. "I wouldn't dare because you'd do anything to avoid it. Especially once you find out what it is. But fear not, while it will be scary, it will turn out to be the best thing ever. If you're not a dumbass about it. " The enigmatic statement didn't reassure.

"You're not making sense," he grumbled.

"Because you asked me to not say anything. Fear not, you'll soon see." Elspeth clapped her hands and rocked on her heels, lost her balance, and landed on her rump. "It's going to be such fun."

"For whom?"

"So convinced everything is bad. Relax. Let yourself feel. It might change your outlook on life."

"I feel." Annoyed. Angry. Maybe a little hungry for that aforementioned pie.

The woman's laser stare pinned him, and he almost squirmed. "You've been holding back for a long time. It's time for you to find what makes you happy. " Elspeth's strange gaze focused on the cat. "And you need to allow it to happen."

Kitty sniffed and turned her head, dismissing the seer.

He completely understood. He wanted to get away as well. "I'm looking for Jeebrelle. She told me to meet her at the Silvergrace property." He'd agreed but only if she promised to do it outside the house. Too many dragonesses lived inside, with more than a few looking for a mate.

Not him.

Never him. A man with his violent past was better off alone.

"Your friend is here." Elspeth went to rise, and he offered the pregnant woman a hand, hoisting her.

"Where?"

"Close by, but you might want to give her a few more minutes since she's spending time with Babette."

"Who I'm also meeting with. Which direction?"

"That way. In the heart of the hedge maze," Elspeth pointed. "But take your time or you might see more than you want, if you know what I mean." She winked.

The implication brought a grimace. It would appear his mage sister had fallen into the same trap as Azrael and Mikhail.

Love.

Nasty emotion. Made smart men do stupid things. He'd never allowed it in his life. Loving things never ended well. It was why he didn't have a hoard like the other dragons. Everything he owned he wore, and if he lost it, then he replaced it.

The cat butted against his hand, and he petted it.

"Oh, my, you're in for such a surprise when you realize you're not as hardhearted as you think." Elspeth giggled as she bloody read his mind.

A grave trespass. "Careful, woman, how you speak to me. Push me and I will kill you."

"Are you threatening my mate?" A gravelly query.

The man who appeared from the shadows could have been dragon with the menace he oozed. And yet...

Israfil sniffed and recognized the scent. Demon. Rare for this world and not someone to trifle with. He inclined his head. "You should teach your woman to mind her tongue."

"My mate's tongue does just fine as is," the man drawled, placing his arm around her.

Elspeth giggled. "Luc, I know what you're thinking, and it's so bad."

"Bad for who? Because it ain't bad for me," the man murmured.

Kitty hacked up a hairball, and Israfil almost joined her. "I'm going to find Jeebrelle." He turned and headed away from the happy couple.

A demon and a dragon. Mating. In his day, that kind of blood mixing never happened. Made him wonder what kind of child they'd have. Probably a strange one.

He found the labyrinth easily enough. The hedges were taller than him, thick with bushy branches, the trails in it tricky—if you didn't have a nose. He easily found Jeebrelle and her companion in the center of it, their hair in disarray and Jeebrelle's dress buttoned improperly. The two women looked flushed and rather pleased with themselves.

It reminded him that he'd not been with anyone since his imprisonment. Still had no interest. Sex led to expectations, either of money or affection. He currently had neither.

"Israfil," Jeebrelle exclaimed, the ends of her pale yellow and green hair swirling. "How unexpected."

"You invited me."

"I didn't actually expect you to show." Jeebrelle suddenly noticed her misbuttoned blouse and blushed bright, whereas Babette smirked.

"Fine, then I'll leave," he grumbled. A good thing he didn't care or the humiliation of her reply might have stung. As it was, it reminded him why he hated pretty much everything.

Except his cat. She understood him.

Kitty once more climbed him and hissed at Jeebrelle. He turned on his heel. A sulky dragon mage might have muttered that he didn't want to come. He preferred a silent exit.

"I didn't say go!" Jeebrelle exclaimed.

He paused.

"If the drama llama wants to leave, then let him. I can think of better things to do, like finish what we started." Babette didn't hide the flirtation in the suggestion.

"Finished? Didn't you, er, um," Jeebrelle stammered.

"Fuck yeah, I did," Babette exclaimed. "But I'm a greedy dragon. I want more."

"Oh," Jeebrelle muttered softly.

When they kissed, Israfil gagged. "Must you do that in front of me?" He came from a time when affection was done in private. Never mind the fact the walls were thin and he heard everything; he had no interest in watching.

"Prude," teased his almost-sister.

"More like some of us are focused on what has to be done." He'd returned to rid the world of Shaitan. It was the only purpose left in his life—along with feeding Kitty.

"The big bad was defeated. We've killed a few of the Shaitan with the God Killer, and Daava, a fount of Jinn information, is now playing for our team. Ain't nothing to worry about," Babette reminded.

"Don't be so sure. I believe the Shaitan have a new plan." His ominous prediction.

"Based on what?" Jeebrelle asked. "There are too few left to open a door to the Iblis." The Iblis being an all-powerful being who wanted to eradicate all living things.

"Just a feeling." He couldn't really explain it any better than that.

"Try taking an antacid for that or smoking a fat doobie. Because that's just your anxiety talking," Babette suggested. "Let's be real, the worst we gotta deal with is another one of those genies getting loose, and we've got a weapon against that now. Worst-case scenario, we shove it in a bottle."

The downplay of his instinct annoyed. "If you don't want to help…"

"Of course, we do," Jeebrelle soothed. "Why else did I invite you but to further our original mission?"

"Does this mean you know where to find one of the artifacts?" Three thousand years ago, seven Shaitan had been imprisoned. Now, all but a few had been released. He'd made it his mission to locate and dispose of them.

"As a matter of fact, I do have a possible location. However, it's going to be awkward getting to it."

"Where?" he asked.

"If the research is correct, it's hidden in some

catacombs." Jeebrelle held up a phone. How progressive of her. The screen displayed an image of a stone and bones that could have been located anywhere in the world.

"Where is that?"

It was Babette who replied, "We're going to Paris."

Chapter Two

Paris, the supposed city of lovers.

Blech.

Serafina eyed the couples with their phones and selfie sticks as they posed in front of everything, looking for the perfect shot. It all seemed so fake and forced. She doubted half of those she saw smiling too brightly were even happy with their partner. Being single was so much better, and she'd know. She'd passed the thirty-year mark unfettered. While her friends succumbed to the marriage trap, she barely dated, finding fulfillment instead with her job, which often brought her to interesting places.

Treasure hunter. That's what she liked to call herself, although her business card and website labeled her an acquisitions specialist. She sought rare artifacts from around the world and resold them to people with deep pockets. Her trip to Paris?

A combination of pleasure, since she loved the food, and business, because she was following a lead.

She stood alone at the back of the line to enter the famous Catacombs of Paris, just another tourist with a backpack and sunglasses. She'd bought her ticket already and now just waited her turn to enter the green building that would give her access to the subterranean ossuary. Created during the French Revolution, the old quarries underground started out as a dumping ground for bodies. Later, cemeteries were emptied and the bodies moved into the catacombs, millions upon millions, a practice that didn't stop until 1860. Now the crypt was a tourist attraction.

Movement by her feet made her glance down to see a cat twining between them, a sleek creature who moved past her and the others to the front of the line. The tip of its tail disappeared as it went inside the building.

Must be nice to skip ahead. Then again, she wouldn't complain. A cat below ground would be hunting rodents. She had no problem with that. In her line of work, she came across too many of those —and bugs.

Behind her, more people joined the queue, arguing.

"Why must we wait like simple mundanes? Our business is pressing," complained a deep male voice.

"Because, in the human world, you can't just

barge around acting as if you're more important than everyone else," a female replied in soft, dulcet tones.

"But I am more important," he stated with stunning arrogance.

"He has a point, Jeebs," a different female added. "I mean you and Izzy are special compared to the humans."

The use of the word "humans" made Serafina frown. She turned to glance behind her, curious about the people speaking so strangely. They weren't as expected.

For one, they were quite attractive. The male was large, ridiculously so, and wearing a cloak head to foot. The hood was pulled to cover his face so she saw only the squareness of his unshaven jaw. His companions hadn't chosen to wear such a concealing overcoat. The shorter of the two had wickedly curly hair braided with silver ribbon that matched her piercings. Three in each ear, one in the nose, another in the brow, and a glint at the belly button, which peeked between her cropped woolen sweater and torn hip-hugging jeans.

The other woman redefined pale. She wore a frothy gown of light yellow, hinting of green, paired with Roman sandals ill-suited for going underground. Her hair kept moving as if caught in a breeze. Odd since Serafina's hair, and everyone else's for that matter, didn't budge.

EVE LANGLAIS

Her staring didn't go unnoticed.

"Mind your business, woman." The man pointed at her.

Rude. "If you don't want people to listen, then don't be so freaking loud."

Even with his hood drawn, she could see how his jaw tightened. "Impertinent wench."

"Prick." She flashed him a smile and the middle finger.

The pierced woman giggled. "Oh, Izzy, I think you just got told."

"Told what? The woman barely spoke."

To which the pierced woman leaned close and whispered.

He tensed, and his robe rippled strangely. Then he radiated cold, and Serafina got a "don't look at me" vibe.

So she turned away. Mostly because the line shuffled forward.

The trio at her back quieted, only occasionally murmuring amongst each other. Straining didn't help her decipher any of it. As if she cared.

When she finally entered the green building and entrance to the catacombs, she saw no sign of the cat. But there were lots of stairs—one hundred and thirty-one according to the website she'd visited—and too many folks. As people slowly descended, she found herself abruptly halted and the man behind bumped into her.

20

The heat of him hit her, as did his scent. She couldn't have described it given its lack of familiarity, but she enjoyed it. It was also a reminder that it had been a while since she'd dated anyone, her last beau being an asshole who asked her to marry him and, when she said no, robbed her. She got her stuff back with interest. And then called the cops on him. Jerk. That was… Shit, five years now?

The man who'd bumped her shifted quickly away. Good, or she'd have told him in no uncertain terms to give her space.

They shuffled down a few more steps, and it happened a second time. She'd have sworn she heard him suck in a breath. She almost looked. Instead, she held still. He remained close a moment longer than before.

"Clumsy human," he muttered and switched places with one of his female companions. She managed to not crowd Serafina at all.

It took forever to make it to the bottom, where someone was in full-blown panic, crying and wailing. Like why come underground if afraid of closed-in spaces? Idiot.

As people hurried away from the hysterical man, others crowded closer to get a video. Serafina used that distraction to head for the spot she'd scouted ahead of time. It took hours of browsing people's personal accounts to figure out where she could hide. Unlike the tourists, she'd come here for a reason, and it didn't involve pretending to be scared and taking pictures.

She located the tucked-away alcove and hid out of sight long enough for the catacombs to empty as they closed for the night. She avoided the security guard who did a quick pass for stragglers.

Soon after, with the place emptied, Serafina emerged from her hiding spot, a creepy one lined with bones. Someone very sick had taken the dead and made them into art. Why? She wasn't sure she wanted to know.

Taking a quick peek at the map on her phone to refresh her memory, she retraced her steps to one of the many locked gates. For safety concerns and other reasons, only a limited section of the catacombs was open to the public. The part she wanted required her picking a lock. The hinges creaked more than she liked as she slipped through the gate and shut it behind her without locking it. A treasure hunter knew to keep their exit route as obstacle free as possible because sometimes they had to leave in a hurry.

Following the notes on her phone and using bits of maps she'd cobbled together of the layout, she threaded her way through the passages, hoping she'd find the right one. She'd already tried accessing the location uncovered in her research via some of the illegal entrances dotted around Paris.

Every single one had led to a literal dead end. But she wasn't giving up.

A treasure hunter expected setbacks. It made the payoff that much more satisfying. And this would be the one that padded her nest egg.

The access tunnel she sought appeared a few feet off the ground. The narrow passage went through the rock, the inside of it dark, despite the lit bulb strung just outside it. A deep breath helped her to forget all the horror movies she'd watched. There were no centipedes or scorpions in the hole. This was France, not the Middle East, so maybe spiders, but she could kill those easily. As for rats? Not likely this high off the floor.

Or so she hoped.

Only faint light accompanied her from the chamber she'd left as she wiggled through. Ahead, there was no illumination at all. She couldn't tell how close she was to the next chamber. All she knew was she hadn't yet reached the end of the shaft when the lights went out.

Chapter Three

Israfil and his companions returned after dark to penetrate the catacombs. Earlier, the tunnels had been too full of people. Jeebrelle had talked him out of ripping open the gate blocking the passage they wanted. Something about the humans calling authorities and him getting shot.

As if a mere bullet could stop him. It would take an army to conquer a dragon mage of his power.

Which led to Babette explaining that the Paris police wouldn't fuck around with what they considered a terrorist threat. They would send a veritable army armed with the new combustion weapons that could rapid-fire his ass into tenderized meat.

While he hated to give in to humans and their rules, with great reluctance he'd agreed to their suggestion they return later. Might as well given Kitty meowed in hunger. Once the complaints started, he had little time before she got vicious. He could use a bite, too.

They ate at a place that served a lot of meat and provided cream for his cat, but only after Israfil threatened the chef. The nerve, asking if he'd sell Kitty while stroking his butcher knife. Israfil was more likely to gut the chef and feed his entrails to his cat.

With the attraction closed until morning, Israfil pointed out the flaw with the plan the women concocted. "Explain how exactly we'll be less noticeable now?" The entrance they sought to use was brightly lit, not to mention security cameras outside tracked movement. He'd learned about modern methods of spying since his arrival.

"Give me a second and I'll take care of it." Babette slunk off, leaving him with Jeebrelle.

The silence stretched awkwardly. He'd never been one to talk much. Plus, there was that time in hunt camp… They'd decided they were much better off as friends.

"How are you?" Jeebrelle broke the impasse.

"Here." Barely. He'd yet to truly feel as if he existed in this time and place. The only thing that grounded him? Kitty.

"Have you found a place to live?"

"Yes." No need to mention it was an abandoned hovel. He had been avoiding a return to the only place he used to call home. Why bother, knowing it wouldn't have anyone inside to welcome him?

"You're adjusting to the new world?" Jeebrelle appeared determined to make him converse.

"Meh." He shrugged. There were things he liked, things he hated. He struggled to be more communicative. "You seem to be doing well."

"Better than just well. I'm happy. Make that in love, which I'll admit surprises me. Babette is my complete opposite. But what can I say? She makes me laugh." Jeebrelle's slim shoulders rolled as she offered a rueful grin.

"Why would you want to find a reason to laugh? The world is a dreary place."

"With much good. And so many wonders. Surely even your ornery self can see it?"

He opened his mouth to argue, only she had a point. The food of this time proved plentiful, varied, and delicious. Music had evolved, not all of it good, but he'd discovered something called metal rock, which he really enjoyed. This era also boasted so many books it reminded him of a dream he once had of creating the world's largest library. He'd always enjoyed reading, and now it had become much easier with the advent of printing on thin sheets of paper. Stone tablets were just so hard to carry around.

"Fine, there are some things I don't abhor about this time. But if you ask me, it's got way too many humans." All over the world and multiplying in numbers that boggled the mind.

"Those humans are the reason why the planet has evolved so quickly."

"Too quickly," he muttered under his breath.

"You haven't changed. Still grumpy. Did it ever occur to you that perhaps you'd be less miserable if you allowed yourself to feel joy?"

"I am joyful. See?" He offered her a grotesque smile.

Jeebrelle shook her head. "I pray one day you find something that makes you happy."

The cat chose that moment to climb him and perch on his shoulder. Kitty dug her claws in as sparks in the distance lit up the sky. Darkness followed, the thick blanketing kind as the power for this sector went out.

Babette returned with a grin. "That will take them a while to fix. I took out a transformer thingy for the area."

No electricity meant no cameras and no alarm. Opening the door to the catacombs proved easy. A wiggle of his fingers and magic became a key. With no tourists in their way, they went down the steps quickly this time. Oddly, he missed the sweet-smelling woman that he'd kept jostling into. A clumsy moment he couldn't explain. It didn't help he enjoyed brushing against her. Even her feisty attitude appealed. Usually, once women understood his greatness, they were too in awe to truly speak their mind.

More than likely, if she'd known whom she addressed—the great dragon mage, Israfil—she'd have behaved differently. Perhaps even gotten to her knees. It had been three thousand years since a woman chose to pleasure him that way.

Picturing it led to him thumping his cock. Not now. Not here. Not her. A good mantra that fought against the way her scent seemed to hover and beckon as he navigated the tunnels, a weak ball of mage light floating ahead of him. Something about the catacombs really dulled his abilities. But he didn't let it worry him. He hadn't come here to fight, although he wouldn't be averse to killing something.

The locked gate he sought had the human woman's essence all over it. He didn't need Jeebrelle saying, "It's unlocked," to know it had been tampered with.

It was Babette who made the next connection. "Is it me, or do I smell that chick you were flirting with?" Babette leaned in and sniffed. "Shit, she went through here and not that long ago. Dude, don't tell me you've been following her trail this entire time? I thought we were artifact hunting."

"We are. The fact she might have passed through is a coincidence."

"Sure it is," Babette drawled. "It's okay, big guy.

You're horny, and for some reason, you like a girl who tells you to fuck off. I totally get it."

"I don't like her," he practically yelled. "Can you stop talking? We have important matters to attend."

Apparently, the silver couldn't remain quiet. "If you were so interested, why didn't you get her name and number while we were in line?"

He turned his darkest look on Babette. "I am not interested in a human."

She didn't cower at his displeasure. Damned modern dragons. "Why not?"

"I would have thought the word *human* said it all." He injected enough disdain to make his preference clear.

"Dude, I've known dragons like you, the kind who claim to hate humans, and guess what? The love bug got them all."

"I highly doubt I have anything in common with anyone you know." Greatness couldn't be duplicated. As to an insect that caused affection? Dragons were immune to most poisons.

"If you say so." The woman rolled her eyes and laughed. "So is your human chick still down here, do you think? Because I smell her going in, but nothing coming out."

"Don't care, because she's not our target."

"Of course, she's not." Jeebrelle settled a hand on his arm. "Do you know where to go? I can't sense anything since we descended."

While it pained him to admit, he wasn't about to lie. "There is something in these tunnels that is muffling my magic."

"Same," Jeebrelle added. "Makes me think of our prison."

The reminder almost brought a shiver. Three thousand years he'd spent in a network of tunnels with twelve others. Not that he'd spent much time with them. The whining got on his nerves.

"It is possible these tunnels once served a similar purpose. They're definitely more than human made." It might have mundane bones patterned into the walls, but he'd seen signs of others having a hand—or a claw—in their design. The way some of the bones were laid formed ancient runes, and he sensed a lingering hint of something, possibly magical, and yet not at the same time.

"If you're not following the girl, and you're not using magic, then where the fuck are we going?" Babette demanded.

Kitty chose that moment to meow impatiently.

"Coming," he muttered, resuming his tracking of a swishing tail.

"Wait, you're following the cat?" Babette's incredulity shone through.

"Kitty is special." He'd known it from the moment he'd spotted her waiting for him.

"I wouldn't have taken you for a cat kind of guy.

How do we know she's not on the trail of a giant rat?"

"We don't." Kitty oftentimes had her own agenda, usually in regard to her feeding. She also had an uncanny intuition of where to go and when, such as when he'd been in the forge when Daava emerged in a human form and that moment on a rooftop when the God Killer came into existence.

A stave he'd borrowed from Azrael.

Babette never shut up. "Anyone else wondering why your chick seems to have gone ahead of us? Is she hunting the artifact, too?"

"Doubtful." Their clue as to its location came from ancient archives that humans couldn't access. AKA crumbling scrolls that hadn't been transcribed until now.

Still even he had to wonder when they stopped at a wall inset with an opening in which Kitty sat. The woman had definitely passed through.

Babette gripped the edge and lifted herself for a peek. "It's a tunnel. And guess what I smell."

"Don't care." Not entirely true. He did wonder at the coincidence of them both seeking out the same location.

"I'll see what's on the other side." Babette quickly wiggled through, but rather than shout, she spoke mind to mind with Jeebrelle.

He didn't allow that kind of familiarity in his

own head and had to wait for Jeebrelle to relay what her lover saw.

"She says the chamber on the other side is clear but your female definitely passed through and recently."

"She's not my female," he seethed.

But that wasn't his biggest problem.

Babette said it aloud. "Dude, your steroid-riddled ass will not fit in that hole."

Indeed, his broad shoulders couldn't shove past the tight stone walls.

"We'll have to find another path," she declared.

"Don't be foolish. You and the silver will go through the passage. I will seek a way around."

"Are you sure?"

"Kitty will show me another path." He glanced at his cat, who flicked her tail.

"Be careful, Isra." A shortened name he liked much more than Babette's annoying Izzy.

Careful? He'd lived more than three thousand years. It would take more than a tunnel to kill him.

His feline led him down passages that seemed much too travelled judging by the scents that passed through and those lingering. The secret section surely wouldn't be in these very public places. However, what choice did he have but to follow?

His cat led him to a dead end that appeared empty if one ignored the bones embedded into the wall. His cat sat and looked at him expectantly.

"There's nothing here."

Kitty glanced at the wall then him, arching her head.

"Is there something beyond it?"

Yawn.

He placed his hand on the boney surface. Brittle, yet still firmly attached. What to do? He still wouldn't fit in the other passage, and he'd been so confident in his feline.

"Meow." Impatience hung in the complaint.

"If you're sure…"

The cat moved to the side and waited.

He chose a spot and punched.

Chapter Four

The lights went out, plunging the cavern into darkness. Luckily Serafina had come prepared. The flashlight was in her pocket, and with only a little swearing, she pulled it out. She felt better with some light.

The pant-pissing moment came later as she marked her passage through the next series of tunnels. She could have sworn she heard stone cracking and swung her flashlight around, wondering about—and yes fearing—a cave-in. She glanced overhead and at the walls. As if she'd be able to tell if the whole thing would come crashing down. She had to hope something that lasted this long would continue to for a while longer.

No sifting dust, no apparent cracks, and a breath heaved out calmed her racing pulse. Time to get going. Her phone had the schematic of this section. Supposedly. It turned out to be only partially accurate. Despite following it, she came across a junction that shouldn't exist and a hallway that ended before expected. Given the setbacks, she proceeded to wing it, chalking her turns so she wouldn't get lost when she went to leave, which would happen sooner or later.

Logically, she knew there wasn't anything to fear down here. The dead weren't about to start clawing at her clothes or flesh. A tsunami of rats or bugs happened only in the movies. A cave-in? Possible, but again, not likely given how structurally sound everything seemed and Paris didn't usually have to worry about earthquakes.

Tell that to the trepidation in her stomach. Each step she took she cursed her treasure-seeking spirit. It wouldn't be the first time. She had gone to many places in search of things that were supposedly lost. In some cases, she never found them despite the best clues. On other occasions, she came away with more than expected. It all came down to luck and nerves of steel, very much needed to navigate tunnels plastered literally with the dead.

With every twist, she thought, *It can't be much farther now.* The hope kept her walking, her pace rapid, her light bobbing. She held it high and thus was able to grasp the size of the chamber she entered by the fact she couldn't see the ceiling. The room spread vast enough her light didn't reach the walls either, and she could only see partway across the underground lake. The body of water lay still and dark, the surface of it settled about an inch below the stone lip. She couldn't tell how deep, but it actually proved to be a positive sign, as her clues mentioned the treasure being near an underground lake.

Had she found the correct body of water? She hoped so, and in positive news, it did have passage across. A narrow stone bridge, old, supported by arches that went into the murky depths. The stone was crumbled in places. Would it hold her weight?

She lifted a foot to test its sturdiness when an unexpected and deep male voice froze her.

"I wouldn't if I were you."

Whirling, she brandished her flashlight as if it would protect her. The cloaked stranger from earlier in the day materialized in the tunnel she'd just exited. While his appearance shocked, the incongruous part was the cat perched on his shoulder, eyeing her with disdain.

"You!" she exclaimed. "Why are you following me?" And did she have time to grab her can of pepper mace? It was buried in her backpack because she hadn't expected to be assaulted this deep in the catacombs.

"What makes you think I'm following you?"

"Seems kind of obvious."

He snorted. "Do you always have such a vaunted opinion of yourself?"

"Why else would you be here?"

"Because I have business."

"What kind of business other than harassing women?"

"Again, you act as if you're worth my attention or time."

"Don't even think of touching me. I took Judo." Actually, she'd indulged in a variety of fighting techniques. Blame being attacked on the subway when she was twenty-five. She'd barely escaped a guy who thought she'd be easy pickings. Being a victim stuck in her craw, so she'd gone out and learned self-defense, and wherever she went she had a can of pepper spray.

The stranger pushed down his hood and showed a visage that didn't appear impressed with her claim. Then again, given his size, he probably didn't often encounter anyone who could best him. But as her sensei taught, technique not size was what mattered. Men never understood that whether it be in a fight or bed.

"You shouldn't be here," he declared, his dark brows drawing close. They contrasted against his olive complexion. Middle Eastern, she'd wager. Clean shaven, square jawed, with eyes that appeared to flash silver.

"I could say the same. And I'll add, I was here first."

"There is danger in these tunnels."

"Are you threatening me?"

"Are you always this paranoid?"

"It's called keeping myself safe from stalking creeps."

His lip curled. "Stalking would imply interest, and I assure you you're not worth my time."

Ouch. That might have hurt, especially coming from such a handsome guy, but looks didn't matter when faced with an absolute asshole.

"Listen, here, asswipe, I don't know who you are or why you're following me, but you need to leave."

"Not until I get what I came for."

She brandished her flashlight. "And I already told you, I'll fight if you touch me. And I'll bite, too." She bared her teeth.

He blinked. "Are all human females so violent?"

"Only when threatened." She wondered at his calling her human. Given his slight accent, she chalked it down to English being his second language.

"And once more, since you're apparently slow, I'm not here for you. I'm looking for something."

It hit her with sudden clarity. "You're here for the treasure!"

A cunning expression crossed his features as his

cat leapt to the floor. "What treasure do you speak of?"

Too late she realized she'd admitted too much. So she lied. "The markets will pay good money for old bones from a supposedly haunted ossuary."

"You're lying."

How did he know? "What are you looking for?"

"Something that was lost. And since I'm sure you'll ask, more specifically, a ring."

His reply cemented they both sought the same object.

"As if any grave robbers would have left something like that behind," she scoffed.

"This ring is special and well-hidden for a reason. You'd do well to forget you ever heard of it and leave now."

Wait, was he seriously telling her to take a hike? "Like fuck. It's mine."

"You have it?"

She almost lied but then thought better of it. He did outweigh her, and if he attacked, she might never be discovered. "I don't have it yet. But I'm not leaving until I find it. Alone. So go look somewhere else." She turned back to the bridge, that scary beam of stone.

"You really don't want to do that."

She flashed him the middle finger as she girded herself to cross.

"If you try and cross that bridge, you'll die before you reach the other side. "

She cast him a glare over her shoulder. "Thanks for the vote of confidence. I'll have you know I have excellent balance."

"Won't matter. I'll wager you don't even make it halfway." He swept a hand at the lake, indicating the far side.

"I can swim."

"You're just determined to kill yourself, aren't you?"

She snorted. "You're just saying that because you're too big and clumsy to make it across."

He shook his head. "And to think your species has survived this long."

Okay, that couldn't be blamed on a language barrier. He was being plain rude. The fact he remained convinced she'd come to harm didn't help her nerves any either. Her reply was sour. "Thanks for the warning. Now fuck off."

"If you're too stupid to listen to my warning, then you deserve whatever happens." He shrugged.

"Your arrogance is stunning."

"I would say the same about your stubbornness, woman."

"My name is Serafina, asshole." With that, she turned her back on him to face the bridge. The tenuous link didn't inspire confidence and the murky water below even less.

As if to mock her hesitancy, the damned cat chose to cross it, padding casually, tail waving, disappearing from sight.

The bridge handled it just fine. Serafina only weighed a few more pounds—okay about a hundred and thirty more pounds. Still this expanse had obviously been built for foot traffic. Even if it did collapse, she could swim. Just don't swallow anything because, who knew what kind of bacteria lurked? With that in mind, she put a foot on the bridge.

Nothing happened. She placed a second on the slim stone expanse and didn't realize she held a breath until she released it. She almost turned a triumphant smirk on Izzy, whose name she recalled from earlier and still thought a horrible name for a hunk.

She kept walking, her flashlight lighting her next step. No sign of creaking, cracking, or crumbling. She'd reached the midpoint when she noticed the ominous swirl of water just under the next section.

Probably drainage causing a whirlpool effect.

She heard a grunted, "Fuck," just as a tentacle thrust from the water and knocked her off the bridge.

Chapter Five

The stupid woman ignored his warning. What happened next was entirely her fault.

A tentacle whipped from the lake and knocked her clean off the bridge. She hit with a splash, too startled to even cry out. An arm flailed. The top of her head sank along with the rest of her. The water churned in the spot she got dragged under, and stilled, her sinking light pinpointing the location of her soon-to-be grave.

She should have listened.

"Meow." Kitty waited on the opposite side.

He stepped on the bridge and, within two paces, sighed.

Fuck.

He dove in. The murky depths made visibility difficult. His magic refused to work, and so he relied on senses alone, which led him down, not as deep as some places he'd swam nor as cold. The feeble light provided a beacon to follow.

When it went out, he then went by the memory of the light's general location. He kicked for it, encountering a spongy, yet sturdy tentacle. He grabbed it and wrestled for a moment before deciding on a better course of action.

He pulled forth his sharp spear and stabbed at the spongy body. Azrael would have beaten him if he'd seen Israfil using the God Killer to save a human. In his defense, it worked really well at poking the bulbous beast guarding the lake.

He felt more than saw as the human's body was released, the churning of the waters keeping her from sinking.

By instinct alone, Israfil grabbed hold of her limp arm, and wondered if she was dead. She didn't move at all.

The monster wasn't done yet. It tried to grab hold of him and one-armed, his lungs tight, Israfil thrust and poked until the beast finally retreated. Only then could he kick to the surface, dragging her behind him. They emerged from water to air, and he couldn't tell if she breathed.

Israfil swam to the far side of the lake and heaved her onto the stone. His cat protested with a yowl at the droplets that hit her fur. He pulled himself up after the woman and grimaced at his soaked clothes. His power might be weak in this place, but there was enough to sluice himself dry.

Then he put his hand on the woman, drawing the water from her lungs by magical force. It spilled from her lips in a dark torrent. When no more appeared, he leaned back on his haunches and waited.

It took a second before the woman—who'd called herself Serafina—coughed and spewed. She rolled onto her stomach and spat the brackish water. Gagged a bit, too.

He waited until she'd managed a few shuddering breaths before saying, "Told you it was dangerous."

She flipped her sopping hair out of her face and glared at him. She'd lost none of her spirit apparently. She snarled in a voice hoarse from coughing, "Thanks for the warning. I guess you expect thanks for saving me."

"You'd not have required rescue if you'd listened."

"I didn't expect—" she waved a hand—"a friggin' octopus in the sewer."

His brows lifted. She'd mistaken a kraken for a mundane creature that was quite delicious when deep fried and dipped in sauce. Kitty preferred hers raw. The human should count herself lucky the confines kept the beast smaller than its ocean-faring brethren.

"These catacombs were abandoned with good reason," he admonished and almost grimaced. For a moment, he'd sounded like his long-dead father. Israfil, too, had gone poking in places he shouldn't and almost paid the price.

"Yeah, well, they can go back to being abandoned after I find what I came for." She'd somehow retained her knapsack and shrugged it off and rummaged. She emerged with a new flashlight that worked when she pressed a button.

"Are you sure it's worth it?" Asked quite honestly given the bluish pallor of her lips and the shivering of her wet frame.

"You tell me, Izzy, since you're after the same thing."

"My name is Israfil, not Izzy."

"Don't care."

They glared at each other. And something strange happened. Heat unfurled inside him. Desire.

Need.

For the first time in a long time, Israfil found something he actually wanted.

The feeling was not returned.

Serafina got to her feet and made a face at her damp clothes. "Ugh. This is going to suck."

He could have dried them, but he'd been told to not do magic in front of the humans. Something

45

about being captured and dissected if he was caught.

"Maybe you should leave and change."

"You'd like that wouldn't you? Then you could have the treasure all to yourself," she accused.

He could have told her flat-out she wouldn't get the ring no matter how much she searched. Instead, he kept quiet. She'd soon realize the folly in continuing her search.

"That dip better have been worth it," she grumbled as she squished her way to the back of the chamber where a pedestal sat, the surface of it empty. Her light bobbed over it, and yet that didn't prove to be her destination. She moved to the back wall and ran her hands over the smooth stone.

He admired her spirit, even as he already knew no secret mechanisms hid in this chamber.

"Where is it?" she muttered.

"Where is what?"

"There should be a doorway."

"You mean this one." Having joined her, he rapped on a section. "It appears to have been sealed shut."

"Says you."

"Did you really think the ring would be so easy to find?" he taunted. "If it were, someone would have already retrieved it."

"Thanks for stating the obvious."

He pressed his lips into a line. "We'll need to find another route."

"There is no 'we.' You want to give up? Go. I'm not done looking." She kept groping the wall, and jealousy filled him.

Which made no sense. Why should he care what she touched?

She rapped her knuckles against the stone. Since she lacked magic or dragon strength, he wasn't sure what she hoped to accomplish.

"Without a hammer of some kind, you won't be able to pound your way through. It's solid rock."

"I can see that," she snapped, kicking the wall in frustration. A kick not strong enough to do anything, and yet, they heard an audible crack.

Not as worrisome as the fine silt that suddenly dusted them from above.

She aimed her flashlight overhead to reveal a fissure. It spread as they watched. Her eyes widened.

"Uh-oh."

Finally, she showed common sense.

"We should leave." He found himself grabbing her hand and tugging.

She didn't protest as they ran for the bridge. As she put a foot on it, the first overhead chunk hit the floor behind them with a thud that proved ominous.

"Move faster," he admonished, getting on the bridge behind her. Crossing it would be faster than swimming, but also more dangerous, as there was nowhere to go other than the water if the ceiling chose to come down on them.

She moved quickly, following his cat in the lead, only to shriek as the bridge in front of her exploded as a rock fell on it and smashed a section. They had no time for her hysterics. He grabbed her around the waist and leaped to the remaining section. Holding her even once he landed, Israfil raced across the bridge amidst spraying water from falling debris.

They hit the far shore, but they weren't yet safe.

The trembling and cracking followed them as they ran through the tunnel, a burst of speed at the end of it sending them into the next room just in time as the corridor collapsed.

Dust billowed, obscuring her feeble light. Hearing her cough, he did a bit of magic, enough to draw the dirt away from her lungs and give her room to breathe. A kindness he didn't understand.

When the air calmed, in a voice quite hoarse, she said, "I need a drink."

And apparently, he wasn't invited.

Chapter Six

Once they departed the underground catacomb—a lovely place with so many delicious scents—Kitty's servant stared after the female for longer than she appreciated. Admiration should be directed at her at all times. However, she forgave her servant given she could smell the mating fever upon him. Once he satisfied the heat in his loins, he would better fulfill his duties, such as feeding her.

In the meantime, until he came to his senses, she had to resort to meowing for his attention.

He glanced down. "What's wrong, Kitty?"

Obviously starvation. She uttered her dissatisfaction, and he scooped her up, perching her upon his shoulder. At least he knew how to properly carry someone of her stature.

"After all that commotion, I think we could both use some food."

An excellent plan, except for the fact his steps headed in the same direction the woman took. He couldn't follow for long, as the street they entered with its many spicy wares obliterated the female's scent.

Her servant went a little farther than Kitty liked —past that delicious place smelling of fish—before he realized he'd lost the trail of the female. But Kitty forgave him when he offered her a saucer of warm cream and oily anchovies. She purred as she ate, sitting on the cushions piled to bring her to the right height at the table. Because, unlike the strays of the street, she was civilized.

Funny how much she grasped since her second wish to understand. What she'd gained went beyond simple knowledge and included perception of two-legged behavior. Her brilliant mind deduced her servant needed her help and for more than one reason.

Firstly, he sought more of the Shaitan, specifically the remaining trapped ones. Like the one she'd freed from the bottle and who still owed her a wish. It had fled, but the wish that bound them remained.

The nearest accessible Shaitan would be the one hidden in the underground lair. It was that scent she'd used to lead them, a route no longer available since the female ruined it. Then again, that path might not have been feasible for the two-legged because only Kitty would have fit in the sluicing duct. Given the warren of tunnels underground, Kitty already knew there was another way to it. She'd gotten a whiff as they'd passed a sewer grate.

"Meow." In that one rolling sound, she told him exactly where they had to go.

Being dumb, her servant didn't understand. She really needed someone to translate her wisdom. Her intelligence was being wasted, which was how she suddenly saw, with perfect clarity, how to fix a few problems at once: her human's fixation on the female, the location of the next artifact, and the need for him to understand she should be fed more often. How hard was it for him to constantly offer her treats before she wasted from starvation?

Time for her last wish. The Shaitan Kitty had freed could have been close or far; it didn't matter once she made her final request.

Kitty meowed her demand, and then she licked her cream dish dry before attacking the dirt on her hindquarter, lifting her leg gracefully and laving the entire area. Lick. Slick. Long lave. Nuzzle.

Her servant, consumed by awe at being allowed to watch her in regal action, growled, "Must you do that in public?"

Chapter Seven

The bottle of booze Serafina bought sat untouched on the dresser as she paced her hotel room. Today hadn't gone as expected at all. And it was more than just the fact she'd failed to retrieve the treasure she sought, almost got drowned by seafood, and crushed in a cave-in.

Who the hell was the man who'd rescued her? Izzy. Short for Israfil. A man who dove into a dirty lake to save her from an octopus—that didn't belong in the middle of Paris—which, in her panic, she'd mistaken for a monster. Blame the creepy catacombs with the skulls all over the place, staring at her. It made her imagine things, such as Israfil somehow remaining dry after his dip.

Perhaps his cloak repelled water? It didn't explain his hair or the fact the exposed clothing underneath remained dry, unlike her, the sodden rat. Her hair hung in damp clumps. The moist reek of it was a reminder she'd almost died. It made her rethink her decision to go after the treasure.

Collect an artifact from an underground tunnel system. Sounded easy until she almost died twice. Hopefully the third time wouldn't be the charm, because she wasn't giving up quite yet.

Next time, no crossing dubious bridges over murky underground lakes and no kicking of seemingly solid walls. She still shuddered to think how close she'd come to being buried alive. She had Israfil to thank for her life. Jerk. She hated being beholden.

As she shivered, it occurred to her that she risked getting sick if she didn't strip out of her damp clothes and get rid of the filth coating her. She emptied her pockets first. Her phone would have to be replaced. Hopefully she wouldn't lose any information when she swapped the SIM.

She emptied her knapsack, most of the items garbage now that they'd got wet. She'd need to get a spare waterproof flashlight—because only idiots went cave exploring with just one—and a new can of pepper spray. Would that have worked against a tentacle? Maybe a machete would be better. Which led to her thinking of zombies. Hard not to, having seen firsthand the skulls and bones embedded in the walls. If, on her next visit, they started rattling or snapping their teeth, she might just lose her mind.

Her clothes hit the floor in a heap as she headed for a well-deserved hot shower. The older hotel satisfied with a steaming stream that left her skin pink and finally removed the chill within.

She'd brought a robe on the trip, knowing how little hotel towels could be. She hated getting dressed right after a nice shower. Air drying did a body good. She slid on the oversized terry cloth, sashed it, and then towel wrapped her hair. To her surprise, she still didn't want a drink of her hooch; rather she craved food. And her dumb ass didn't think to grab any.

Suddenly starving, she ordered sushi from a restaurant downstairs as a fuck-you to the sea critter that tried to make her its meal.

When someone knocked, she assumed it was the delivery guy. It turned out to be unexpected company.

She opened the door to Israfil holding a paper bag. He was still wearing his dark cloak with the cat from the catacombs on his shoulder. A sleek feline with staring eyes. Unnerving as it looked at Serafina almost as intently as Israfil.

She gathered herself. "What are you doing here? Are you stalking me?"

He snorted. "Hardly."

"Then how did you find me?"

"Kitty led me." His ridiculous reply before he pushed his way in.

It should be noted she could have stopped him; however, as he passed, she'd have sworn the cat spoke in a very feminine, high lilt.

"I told you the female was here," it drawled smugly. "And she is obviously expecting me. I smell goodies in that bag."

Serafina's gaze dropped to his hand and the sack it held.

He thrust it at her. "I believe this is your dinner."

Which led to the cat uttering a shocked, "*Her* dinner? I'm the one starving." Followed by a sighed, "It's so hard to find good help these days."

"Um." Serafina blinked. She'd not taken Israfil for the type to joke, and yet not only was he pranking her, he also had excellent ventriloquist skills.

He whirled in the tight space and, seeing no table, set the bag on the dresser alongside her soggy items. "Okay, Kitty. We're here. Now what?"

"Someone needs to give me whatever smells so good." The cat opened its mouth and appeared to actually speak.

It was really a well-done act. Serafina clapped. "Bravo. You should take that routine to the stage. Then again, you're in Paris. You might make more money on the streets with tourists."

His brows pulled together. "What insanity are you blabbing now, woman?"

"I told you, my name is Serafina."

"I don't really care," he grumbled.

"Then why are you here?" Annoyance overtook her Stockholm syndrome pleasure at having an actual hunky stalker come looking for her.

"Because Kitty can be most insistent. Since her instincts are usually good, I tend to listen."

"Actually, the problem is you don't listen," the cat complained. "If you did, I wouldn't need this *female*"—a sniff in her direction—"to translate."

"I don't know why you feel a need to pretend your cat is talking, but gotta say it's weird. As in, I think you should leave before I call the police." Because she might be able to fight, but crazy people could be strong. Serafina wished her pepper spray hadn't stopped working after its dunk. Then again, would it even work against the big lug?

"Hold on, are you saying you can understand Kitty?" He glanced at the feline then Serafina. "What is she saying?"

The cat yawned. "She is saying that you're both idiots who need to start paying attention."

"She says you're an idiot, which I agree with."

He scowled. "Now I know you're lying. Kitty adores me."

"Sure she does, and I'm done with your dumb game. Stop pretending. I know it's you faking that your cat can talk."

"My cat doesn't speak!" he insisted.

"Tell him I know how we can still get to the artifact despite the fact you broke the most direct route," the feline said.

Rather than convey that message, Serafina snapped, "It's not my fault that room collapsed. And it wasn't as if there was a way past the solid stone walls."

"Guess we'll never know since you ruined that route." The cat sniffed. "Now we'll have to go a different way because I am not wading through water. Nasty stuff." The feline shivered.

"Excuse me, your majesty," she drawled.

"Fuck me, you are talking to Kitty." Israfil sounded surprised.

She turned a glare on him. "Enough with the act. I know you're throwing your voice."

"Why would I toss it?" He frowned.

"Fuck off already. If you have something to say, just say it."

He jabbed a finger in her direction. "You're the one claiming my cat is talking. Not me. All I hear is meowing because Kitty is probably hungry again. Despite her diminutive size, she eats quite a bit."

At his stubborn rebuttal, she glared. "Get out."

"Why are you angry? Is it your womanly time?" he cajoled.

He did not just say that.

"I can't believe he said that." The cat glanced at Israfil. "Are you going to slap him, or shall I?"

"Go ahead," Serafina offered. She didn't actually expect the cat to swipe and snarl. But Kitty did, scoring three bright scratches on his cheek before she jumped to the bed and dug her claws in to tug the blanket into a pile for her new perch.

Israfil ignored the marks on his cheek to growl, "See if I get you warm cream in the morning."

"Oh, you'll get me the cream *and* some fresh fish as an apology for your impertinence." the feline replied and gave her paw a lick before slicking it over her head.

It would have been funny if it wasn't so weird.

Israfil stomped for the door. "I'm leaving."

"Aren't you forgetting something?" Serafina asked.

"Kitty knows how to find me if she wants to." The door slammed shut.

"Don't worry. He'll be back. I own him."

Serafina stared at the cat. That still talked even with him gone.

"How is this possible? Are you wearing a microphone?" She patted the cat, who tolerated it for a moment before swiping and sprinting away to climb atop the headboard.

"Watch how you're touching me, human. Have you never been taught how to properly pet a goddess before?"

"You're really talking to me, aren't you?" Serafina whispered, eyes wide.

"Yes, and, so far, really not enjoying it. I blame your inferior mental incapacity. To think I wished to have you as my translator."

"You did what?"

"Let me say it slowly so you understand," the cat enunciated. "I had three wishes from the Jinn I freed. The first got me out of danger. The second gave me awareness. And the last gave me you, which, in retrospect, might have been a colossal waste."

Serafina ran for the apartment door in time to see the stairwell door closing. "Get your ass back here, you giant lug!"

She thought she'd have to chase him down, but Israfil reappeared. "You'd better not be addressing me!"

"Your cat is fucking talking." She couldn't help the expletive.

"So you claim." He sounded skeptical.

"Because she really is. She said something about wishes and freeing a Jinn."

His brows rose. "Kitty can speak?"

"Wait, you mean you can't understand her?"

"Our communication is done without words." He sounded almost defensive.

"Well, I'm getting actual vocal stuff, and it is freaking me out. Like why would your cat choose me as its translator?"

"Because if I must endure you, then you should

be useful," came the haughty reply from behind her.

Serafina whirled and glanced down to see the cat sitting by the hotel room door. "Who says you have to endure me?"

"Since the dragon wants to mate with you, I'm afraid you'll be around for a while."

Chapter Eight

K itty meowed at Serafina, and Israfil could only watch as they conversed, a one-sided conversation that ended with Serafina wide-eyed then laughing.

"What is so amusing?"

"Your cat thinks you're horny for me." She snickered.

His recent foray into language translated the unfamiliar word as lusty.

His turn to gape. "I am not." A lie. He'd been aware of the human from the moment she opened the door wearing a long robe, the sash tied in a bow that would be so easy to undo.

Her hair, bound in a towel, showed off the smooth column of her throat. He wanted to nibble at that skin. Peek—

He glared at Kitty. "I am not desirous of the female."

"Meow."

"She says you shouldn't lie. And would someone feed her? She's starving." Serafina offered him a reproachful look. "No wonder she came looking for me. Poor hungry thing."

"I just fed her!"

"You know they need to eat more often than us because of their tiny stomachs. Come here, sweetheart." Serafina scooped up Kitty and placed her on her shoulder. His cat appeared quite smug.

He, on the other hand, had hit bemusement. What was happening here? His cat could speak?

As they re-entered Serafina's abode, he asked, "What did Kitty say about wishes?"

"She said she freed a Jinn and got three. One she used to escape some kind of danger. Then she asked to be smart, and apparently, having me be her translator is her third."

"You, not me?" He eyed Kitty, who sat on a dresser licking herself. The apartment was cramped and lacking in a kitchen. "You live here?"

"Not exactly. Just staying here until I find what I came for."

"The ring." He ignored his cat situation to ask the more important question. "How did you know to look in the catacombs?"

"How did you?" she countered.

"Through research."

"Same." Her lips pressed into a line. "What are your plans if you find it?"

"There is no if. I will locate the artifact because, as one of the last of the dragon mages, it is my duty to ensure the Shaitan cannot return and end our world."

Her hand flashed into the space between them. "Hold on and backup. Dragon what?"

"I am a dragon mage. Don't pretend you don't what that is. Humans are aware of our existence, if only recently, according to your news sources."

"You mean the hoax people are debunking," she said with a dismissive wave.

That lifted a brow. "Do I look like a hoax?"

She eyed him up and down. "You look like a man. A weird one in a cosplaying cloak. What are you supposed to be? Jedi Knight? Vampire?"

"Some have nicknamed me horseman of the apocalypse."

"Which one? Plague?"

"That would be my sister, Jeebrelle. I am usually called War." Which he approved of. He'd been quite valiant in battle.

"So you're a dragon mage and a horseman of the apocalypse. How does that work exactly? Do you carry your horse in your dragon claws?" She snickered.

The woman mocked him. She didn't believe. He eyed his cat. "Would you tell her who I am?"

"Meow. Meow. Meow."

Serafina laughed. "Please. There's no way that man"—she pointed—"is a dragon."

Israfil had quite enough of the insolence. He eyed the room briefly before deciding fuck it—one of three new favorite expressions along with "fuck me" and an emphatic "fuck." He conjured a portal, tossed Serafina through it, and, as he followed the tip of his cat's tail to the other side, shifted.

Chapter Nine

One minute, Serafina stood in her hotel room having the weirdest conversation. The next, cold sucked the heat from her as she entered a dark space that stole her breath. It lasted an eternity of a second before she emerged in a desert. Like an actual sandy-dune desert.

She hit the hot sand and fell to her hands and knees. What the ever-loving fuck?

She popped to her feet and realized she wasn't alone. Kitty sauntered out of the black hole, tail up, taking her time, not flinching one bit as a monster came through after her.

Serafina's mouth rounded in horror as she backed away from the massive dragon with its curling horns. It huffed in her direction.

A dragon.

Israfil hadn't lied. Holy shit. He was a dragon!

She sat down hard and remained in stunned place as he crouched in front of her, back in his human shape.

"I am going to guess by your expression you now believe me."

"How does your tiny body get so big?" Her intelligent response.

Indignation had him recoiling. "I am not tiny."

"You weigh what? Two forty? Even if it was way more than that, your dragon had to be over a ton."

He frowned. "What does weight have to do with anything?"

"Science, dude. Shouldn't your mass be the same whether you're a man or fire-breathing dragon?"

"I don't breathe fire."

"That's a bummer. What can you do?"

He stared at her. "Are you actually asking a dragon mage that question?"

"Mage as is in magician?"

He swung away from her and cursed in a language so melodic she wouldn't have known if Kitty didn't shake her head. "Such foulness in the presence of a goddess."

She eyed the cat. "Have you known each other for long?"

"Only since he emerged from his prison."

"He was in prison?" Great, she was in some weird place with a stalking dragon-mage convict.

"Not a real one, so don't act so shocked," Kitty drawled. "More like a self-imposed period of isolation that ended when I broke the first seal."

"Seal for what?"

That led to Kitty explaining the seven Shaitan, evil magical entities, imprisoned in artifacts, a seer who prophesied their return, and the end of all life if the jinn succeeded in their master plan to open a portal to another dimension.

"…and that is how my servant came to find the goddess he'd been waiting to worship his whole life," the cat finished.

"Um…" Serafina really had no words for the level of conceit displayed in one tiny feline.

"Now what's Kitty saying?" Israfil had ceased his pacing and cursing to regard Kitty with his brows drawn low.

"Kitty was just telling me how you were a prisoner for a long time and came back to save the world."

He snorted. "Such a simple summary of the most torturous time in my life. And for what? There is nothing worth saving."

"How can you say that? The world has billions of people."

His jaw tensed. "I don't like people."

"He really doesn't," Kitty confided.

"And yet you're looking for this artifact to stop these Shaitan devils from causing harm."

His scowl deepened. "The illogic doesn't escape me."

"Let's say you do find it, what then?"

"I will destroy the Shaitan within."

"When you say destroy, does it have to be inside the ring when it happens, or can you like get the genie out first and leave it intact?" The practical side of her wanted to know.

"Why does it matter?"

"Because that ring could be worth a lot." As in she could buy a nice place set back from the ocean. Maybe start a normal business that didn't involve skulking in catacombs for treasure.

"Someone wishes to purchase it?" He spun on her. "Who? Why?"

She bit her lip. She might have said too much. "No one yet, but there's always someone looking for rare and exotic stuff. The older the better."

"I care not about the ring so long as the Shaitan within is taken care of."

A dark promise that had her shivering despite the heat and the sun beating down. She glanced around. "Where are we?" She glanced at her feet and hoped this place didn't have those people-eating sand worms from *Tremors*.

"Nowhere anymore. It would seem the city I once knew here has succumbed to time."

"How old are you?"

"Ancient," croaked the cat before she snickered.

"Old enough," he replied.

"I'm thirty-three." Why she volunteered, she couldn't have said.

The corner of his mouth lifted. "I'm almost one hundred times that but have remained around your age in appearance despite my long incarceration."

She did the mental math. "Shit." That was a long time to be in prison.

The baking sun had her fanning herself. "I don't suppose we can head back."

"To that dreary box you call a room?" He grimaced.

"That box has my clothes."

"You are flushed," he observed.

"More like thirsty. I swear that heat sucked all the moisture out of me."

"I can help." His hand on the ground didn't glow or do anything weird, and yet she'd have sworn the Earth trembled. When he removed it, a dark spot appeared. It grew until the water arced in a fountain about two feet from the ground.

She kneeled by it and cupped her hands, slurping at it, amazed by the cool freshness.

As she drank, sand scooped around the fountain hole and hardened enough to contain the filling waters.

More magic. The reality of it had her leaning back on her heels and feeling lightheaded.

He noticed. "Are you going to faint?"

on the bed and curled into a ball with her tail tucked around her frame.

She waited, but the cat really went to sleep. "Your cat is annoying."

"Very. But she is also wise.

"And food obsessed. She said to have something ready for when she wakes. I'd listen to her. She's liable to rip your face off otherwise."

"She can be demanding," he said offhandedly.

"An odd choice of pet for a horseman of the apocalypse. Or is she a dragon snack for later?"

"Too small. We prefer cattle."

That caused her to blink. "The only raw thing I eat is sushi." Which reminded her. She grabbed the bag and, in the blink of an eye, had Kitty rubbing against her.

"Gimme. Gimme. Gimme."

"I thought you were napping."

"Hungry." The cat swiped.

The cat got three pieces, which she destroyed, scattering the rice and seaweed to get at the seafood. Serafina chose to pop entire pieces into her mouth and watched with amusement as Israfil eyed the rolls with suspicion before trying one.

Surprise lit his features. "It's good."

"You've never had sushi?"

"I spent almost three centuries eating rats, spiders, and cave mushrooms. I haven't had a lot of things."

Distaste tugged her lips into a moue. "Couldn't you magic yourself some food?"

"Our curse took our magic from us, leaving behind only the memory of it."

"Sounds awful."

"It was, and yet oddly, despite only being released a short time ago, it feels a distant memory."

Kind of what her mother used to say about giving birth.

"Kitty said there were thirteen of you but not all survived."

"No, many died. I know of only six, including me, who lived to escape."

"Six? I thought there were only supposed to be four horsemen."

"I know little of your legends. You should ask whoever first uttered that prophecy."

"They're long dead, and it's been a part of legend and pop culture for a while." She grabbed the bottle of booze and unscrewed it for a swig before passing it over. She'd given up on getting rid of him and his cat.

"The world has certainly changed." He took a swig. His eyes widened in surprise, and he took a longer draw.

"Did you leave behind family? A partner?" It slipped out before she could stop herself.

"Parents, siblings." He rolled his shoulders. "At the time, we didn't think we'd be captured for so long." He frowned. "I don't know why I'm telling you this."

"It's called conversation. A thing people do when they hang out together."

"I don't hang, as you call it. I should go." He rose.

Blame the booze, but she grabbed for his hand, feeling the heat and the callouses on his fingers. It tingled, and her gaze met his.

"You can't leave." She licked her lips. "Not yet. We still have business to discuss."

"Do we?" He purred the words, his eyes smoldering.

He flirted, and it would have been easy to lean into him and press her mouth to his. Taste him. Instead, she released his hand and looked away.

"We need to talk about the treasure we're both looking for."

"There is no we."

"Are you sure of that? Because seems to me you need me. Your cat made sure of that."

They both glanced at the sleeping bundle, who'd chosen the crevice between the two pillows to sleep.

"It would have been more expedient for her final wish to be everyone understanding her," he grumbled.

"But she didn't, so you're stuck with me." Declared more grumpily than she meant. Blame her offense at how much he wanted to get rid of her.

"I guess I am," he murmured.

"Gee, could you sound any less excited?" She found herself insulted, especially since she'd actually believed Kitty when she said Israfil had the hots for her.

"You'll just get in the way."

"Someone has a high opinion of himself."

"Modesty is for those who aren't as special as me."

"Also really arrogant."

"And?"

"It's not exactly attractive."

He arched a brow. "If that's true, then why can I smell your arousal?"

Chapter Ten

The scent of Serafina's desire had only grown since she'd opened the door. She might verbally spar with Israfil, but it appeared to only deepen her attraction—and his, too. Even now that she'd met his true self, had seen his magnificence, she didn't fear but lusted.

Her jaw dropped. "No, you can't. I'm not— That is—"

"Now who's about to lie?" he taunted.

Her chin lifted as her shoulders squared. "You're mistaken."

"We both know I am not." He stepped closer.

She held her ground, tilting her head farther back, exposing the smooth column of her neck. Her breathing shortened and her eyelids drooped as she licked her lips to say, "I don't like you."

"I don't like you either. But like has nothing to do with arousal."

"That sounds like something an arrogant ass like you would say."

"Are you really going to deny wanting to kiss me?"

"I'd rather kiss the octopus in the cave." She stared stubbornly at him.

The impasse might have lasted forever if they'd not lunged at each other, her grabbing him as he reached for her.

His lips touched hers, and heat erupted. Absolute madness. He lost all reason in that moment. Even forgot he hated humans.

He kissed her, and she embraced him right back, their mouths sliding and caressing. Their breaths shortening. Fingers clutching, squeezing flesh.

He thrust a hand between their bodies and parted her robe, slipping between her thighs to find her moist core. He fingered the slick entrance of her sex, and her hips rocked against him as he stroked. Her panting emerged with short mewls, vibrating sounds he absorbed with his mouth as he kept kissing her. Stroking her. Feeling her tighten and gasp then orgasm on his digits. Her sharp cry caught by his lips.

And still she trembled and groaned, wanting more.

Wanting him.

"Meow."

Serafina flung herself away from him and placed her hands on her red cheeks. "Oh fuck. That wasn't supposed to happen."

She dared to regret!

He growled. "You desire me."

"You're hot, no doubt, but I'm not the kind of girl who sleeps with strangers." She tucked her robe tight.

"Who says we'd be sleeping?" he drawled with all the arrogance he'd earned.

"We are not having sex."

"Liar. You want me inside you."

Her eyes went unfocused before she shook her head. "It's not a good idea."

"Meow."

Serafina glanced at Kitty. "Shut up. I am not having sex with him because you said so."

"Meow. Meow."

"You can order me all you want. Still not happening," she argued with the cat. "It was a momentary lapse of judgment probably caused by breathing in some noxious catacomb fumes. Or maybe it was the water."

She sought excuses to deny what she felt.

Israfil wanted to punch something. Since he couldn't, he flung open the door. "I need air."

He burst out of her room, and this time she didn't call him back. Surely he wasn't disappointed?

Israfil headed up to the rooftop, standing under a clear night sky where he could take deep breaths. They did nothing to help. No amount of pacing or punching concrete could erase the feel of her in his arms. The taste of her on his lips. The scent of her lingered on his fingers.

And what did he do? He licked them and closed his eyes, wishing now that he'd gotten between her legs. Maybe if he'd licked her, she wouldn't have turned away from him. Why did that bother him? Could it be because he'd never been this ardent about a woman? Never wanted more?

He drifted into the past...

Paella waited for him when he left the tavern's main floor. He'd rented the room for one last night. He opened it to see the voluptuous woman lounging on his bed.

He grimaced. "I didn't ask for you."

She patted the mattress. "I hear you're leaving. I thought we'd enjoy one last night."

"It's already been three. I need my sleep."

"Sleep over sex with me?" She'd been insulted, but rather than stomp off, she resorted to pouting and pulling down her blouse. She played with her nipples, and he sighed. "Don't make me toss you out."

In the end, she'd left, and he'd gotten a good night's rest. Although, if he'd have known he'd be sleeping alone for the next three thousand years with only his hand for company, he would have taken her up on the offer.

Maybe he should have been nicer to the women imprisoned with him. That brought a moue of distaste. One didn't fuck one's almost-sisters.

One also shouldn't get involved with a human.

"Argh!"

Thud. He barely felt the skin splitting on his knuckles.

What did it say about him that he wanted to return and kiss Serafina again? He had a strong feeling she'd melt if he truly set about to seduce her.

But then what?

He couldn't exactly leave in the morning. She was the voice for Kitty. He had to keep her around until they at least retrieved the artifact.

Then…

He'd fuck her and leave.

Chapter Eleven

He left and didn't come back. Good, because it was late, and fatigue sucked at every single muscle in her body. Too tired to get into a cat fight over who got the bed, Serafina left Kitty in the middle of the pillows and clung to an edge.

She thought she might have a hard time sleeping. Thankfully, she'd inherited her dad's ability to nod off any time, any place.

It led her into a dream.

She sat on her porch, the one she'd come home to every day after school until she'd moved away to college at eighteen. It burned down during her second year of school with her parents inside. The investigation said they died of smoke inhalation and never felt a thing.

She sure as hell did.

What she didn't understand was why she was rocking in the swing her dad made. She understood she dreamed, and yet, this wasn't a place she'd ever revisited. Too many painful memories.

"Greetings." A nondescript man, his features plain, his suit simple, tipped a bowler hat at her from the sidewalk. "Mighty fine day."

A dream with idle chitchat. Why not?

"It is."

"I don't believe we've met." He approached and held out his hand. "I'm Adevem."

A strange name. She didn't rise to shake his offered hand. "Can I help you?" Because she seriously better not be about to be solicited in her dream. She saw no briefcase, no vacuum cleaner. Maybe he had his religious pamphlets tucked away.

"As a matter of fact, you can. It's come to my attention that you're looking for something special."

Suddenly suspicious, she frowned. "I swear, Israfil, if you're invading my dreams, I will hurt you." She didn't know how, but she'd find out if a kick to a dragon's balls was effective.

The man shook his head with a faint smile. "I am not your dragon companion. But we do come from the same era."

"Who are you?"

"Someone with a warning. Leave the ring alone."

It hit her with a bolt of understanding. Her subconscious obviously had a message. "I already know it's dangerous in the catacombs." She'd almost died, and apparently, it worried her more than she'd realized.

"The catacombs aren't the problem, but the treasure you seek is, as is the one you're partnered with."

Definitely her buried mind reminding her that men shouldn't be trusted.

"I can handle Israfil. And I won't be stopped from getting the ring."

"I wouldn't be so sure of that," he said smugly.

The sky turned dark. The world around her paled to gray. Except for Adevem's eyes. Those glowed as if lit from within.

"Go away." She stood and pinched herself, done with this dream-turned-nightmare.

"Not until you heed my warning. Stay away from the ring, or else…"

The crack of thunder startled her awake, and she lay in bed, staring at the ceiling only faintly illuminated by the glow from lights outside the window.

Her nose wrinkled at an unpleasant smell. Had the cat farted?

A faint scuff had her holding still and listening. The noise came again, as if a foot dragged across the hotel room carpet. Had to be Israfil. Being a man, he most likely went out and got drunk. Now, he'd returned, probably feeling brazen, and because of his blue balls, he'd be demanding. Not his fault she got off and he didn't.

Never mind the fact she should have never kissed him.

She held still on the bed, but Kitty didn't. She woke with a low, warning rumble.

Hunh. Did Kitty not recognize her master?

"Hiss."

That wasn't Kitty, or Israfil. The stench deepened. Not a fart. It was mustier and more putrid. Serafina reached for the lamp. A flick of the switch had her gaping at the creature in her room.

It stood on two legs, but that was where any resemblance to something human ended. It was covered in scales in some areas, fur in others. A mishmash of animal parts that made her brain hurt.

"What is that?" Serafina exclaimed as Kitty rose from her pillow nest with her back arched.

"Trouble."

"No shit," she muttered in reply to the cat.

The monster lunged at her, uttering a sighing moan. She dodged by diving off the bed but had nowhere to go. The thing had her trapped by the wall with the window that offered no escape. Her gaze darted around the room, looking for a weapon.

Unlike dumb horror movies, she knew better than to throw a pillow. The chair would have the right kind of heft. It also weighed more than expected.

She grunted as she tried to lift it high enough to swing.

"Do something!" Kitty demanded.

"I'm trying" she muttered.

The thing shambled closer, its ponderous movements giving her time to rethink her chair strategy. Her gaze lit upon the lamp on the nightstand, the solid brass kind her grandmother used to have. She grabbed hold and pulled, the cord snapping out of the outlet and whipping her in the legs.

"Fuck!" It stung, but she ignored it to swing as the monster came at her again.

A solid whack took off the reaching hand—er, paw? Losing a limb did nothing to deter it.

She swung again so hard that she couldn't stop from smashing the hotel window. Glass tinkled, but she didn't care, or even realize she screamed as she fought for her life—with a useless cat complaining, "Ew, you spattered me."

Chapter Twelve

"There you are. We've been looking for you."

Israfil woke from his reposed state to Babette's irritating voice. He cracked open one eye. "Go away."

"Am I bothering you?"

"Yes."

"Good. Because I'm also bothered by the fact we've spent several hours looking for your annoying butt because Jeebrelle was worried about you."

"I'm fine."

"Obviously, but she didn't know that. She spent over an hour trying to sniff you out of the rubble. Then a few more walking the streets."

"She shouldn't have bothered."

Babette rolled her eyes. "Ah, here we go, the mighty martyr. Nobody loves me. I love nobody. Blah. Blah."

The claim he whined grated, because even he couldn't deny the sulk in his words. "Jeebrelle should have known better. I've survived cave collapses before. She shouldn't allow herself to be distracted from our task."

"Speaking of distraction, how is the stalking of that human going?"

"I am not stalking."

"Then it's just a coincidence you're on the roof of the same hotel as the woman from the catacombs."

"Kitty made me come." It sounded stupid when spoken aloud.

That arched a brow. "Wasn't bestiality a crime in your time?"

His mouth rounded. "I didn't mean—"

Babette snickered. "Dude, your face. Just kidding. Or am I?" Her voice dropped an octave before she cackled.

"Your sense of humor needs work."

"I'm not the one who doesn't know how to laugh. You should try cracking a smile once in a while."

He bared his teeth.

It only made the annoying woman giggle. "Ouch. Someone needs practice. Maybe your lady friend will help you with that. Or is your bad mood because she kicked you out of her bed already?"

He'd never admit to being rejected. "Don't you need to be somewhere else?"

"Nope. I told Jeebrelle I'd find you."

"Congratulations. You found me. Now, go away."

"No can do. I've already told Jeebrelle where we are, and she wants me to stick with you until she arrives."

Damn their mind-to-mind chatter. So much for having privacy so he could sulk in peace. "And how long with that be?"

"Depends, she came across the trail of something she called an *utukku qabri*. Said she wanted to see what it was up to first."

"An *utukku qabri* here?" He rose to his feet. "Where did she sense it?"

Babette cocked her head. "Why are you so interested?"

"Because they are tools of the Shaitan. Human minds and bodies are hard to control, and if an animal or other lifeform isn't available, they'll sometimes resort to animated corpses."

"You're talking about zombies." Babette shook her head. "That is not okay."

"It is the Shaitan way."

"Um, any reason why one of those zombies would be coming for you?"

"Why do you ask?"

"Because Jeebrelle is currently in front of the hotel and says the trail appears to go inside."

That had him glancing at the roof access door, currently closed. "How long ago since it entered?" he asked, rolling his body to limber his muscles.

"Dunno, but she's inside following it. I'm assuming we kill it by bashing in its brains?"

He snorted. "As if they're still controlled by a dead mind. To stop an *utukku qabri* you must take it apart until the animation shatters."

"Sounds like fun."

More like vile, as the rotting parts tended to be squishy and smelly. He dropped a magical sheen over himself to ensure none of it stuck to him. As he waited for the creature to arrive, he heard the distant sound of breaking glass and a scream punctuated by an angry yowl.

In a flash, he leapt over the roof's edge and dropped, cloak billowing, his magic a pulsing presence that slowed his descent enough that he could grab hold of the broken window's edge and vault inside.

Too late to do anything.

The threat had already been conquered. Serafina stood amidst a pile of rotted parts, bent over, gagging.

As for Kitty, she eyed him with reproach and meowed.

Let her complain. His first thought was for Serafina. "Are you okay?"

"Do I look okay?" she snapped, and then she turned her ire on the cat. "Don't eat that!"

Chapter Thirteen

The nerve of her flustered female servant telling Kitty what to do. First off, Kitty gave the orders around here, and secondly, dead thing! Waking up from her nap, Kitty had been delighted at the sight of the rotten corpse.

Of course, the smell proved to be more interesting than the taste. Kitty had pounced on its back and latched on, only to spit out the squishy, rancid meat.

A goddess should only have the freshest of cuts, but that would only happen if her servant survived the attack. With swipes of her paws, Kitty undid some of the ties binding the parts together. Her female servant did a respectable job of smashing those pieces loose.

Her male servant arrived in time to feed her. Only he had the nerve to show up without food.

"Where's my breakfast?" Kitty wailed.

Her wan, two-legged female servant—who'd thrown up on top of the meat, further ruining it—turned her face toward Kitty. "How can you think of eating at a time like this?"

"How can you not? Your stomach is empty. You'll waste away." She could feel herself losing girth as they squandered time talking rather than fetching her sustenance.

The male stomped through guts without getting any of the gore on his cloak or boots. He grabbed the woman by the arms. "What happened?"

"I puked."

"Before that?" he yelled.

"I was sleeping then there was a zombie monster. Which is dead now. I think." The servant glared suspiciously at the floor.

"It's not coming back." He spread his hand and heated the meat, cooking it so that it almost smelled pleasant before it turned into char then ash. Quickly, too. Leaving only the slightest of scorching on the carpet.

The door to the room slammed open. A female rushed in, curly hair bouncing in a fashion that made Kitty want to bat the strands.

"Damn it, I missed all the action."

"So did I," the disgruntled male stated. "The human and my cat took care of it."

The one called Babette eyed the ash on the

floor. "Hope you didn't pay with a credit card because that mess is gonna cost you."

"What mess?" Kitty's male servant snapped his fingers, and a whirlwind siphoned the dust and sent it out of the window.

Pity he couldn't use that skill to bring back a tasty treat.

"Hold on a second. I recognize you. You were in the line yesterday. You know each other," Serafina, with a name almost as fine as Kitty, declared.

"They know each other, but they don't like each other," Kitty declared.

Serafina glanced at her. "Why don't they like each other?"

It was Babette who shout-whispered, "How did that cat talk?"

"By opening my mouth and using my words, imbecile." Kitty put the upstart in her place.

Babette blinked. "Um, excuse me, Kitty, er, ma'am?" She ended on a lilting note of confusion. Probably due to her awe at meeting an actual deity.

"It's Goddess actually, but you may call me Kitty if you pet me." Kitty arched her neck.

"You want me to pet you right now?"

"It wasn't a question."

"Yes, Kitty." Babette leaned forward and stroked her fingers.

"You can understand Kitty?" Israfil blurted out.

"Clear as day, apparently," Babette declared, doing a nice scratch behind Kitty's ears.

"What's clear as day?" Jeebrelle entered and closed the door. "Where did the *utukka qabri* go?"

"If you mean the zombie, it's dead," Serafina declared, still wearing parts of it.

"Don't state the obvious, girl. And how exciting. The whole gang is finally here. Yay." Kitty faked happiness in a dull tone. "Now to the bigger question. Who brought me breakfast? I've been awake for several minutes now, and I still don't see any food."

The servants all stared at her.

The female dragon mage, Jeebrelle, asked, "Why is the cat talking?"

"The better question is, why can you all understand but I can't?" Her male servant turned a glare on his goddess.

Daring to question her will! She rolled a shoulder and flicked her tail. "The women understand because everyone knows male brains are too small to comprehend more than the basics."

Babette coughed and snickered, whereas Jeebrelle gaped. "This is incredible. Is it a spell that allows you to speak?"

"That's a rude question to ask," Kitty pointed out.

"Maybe the cat is cursed. Like that frog in that fairy tale. Do you need someone to kiss you so you can transform back into a human?" Babette inquired.

"Most definitely not. I am perfection incarnate." Kitty lifted her chin. "And I am getting cross. Where is my food?"

"I can't believe you're still whining about that," grumbled Serafina.

"Says the girl who could lick herself for sustenance."

Serafina grimaced. "Thanks for the reminder that I'm wearing dead guts. If you don't mind, I need to shower."

"You do that while we take her highness to breakfast." Babette held out her arms for Kitty. At least she wouldn't have to walk and waste more energy.

Serafina paused at the bathroom door. "Are you coming back?"

"They are because I'm not leaving." Israfil crossed his arms and scowled.

"I don't need you standing guard."

"Says the woman who was just attacked."

"And handled it on my own," she pointed out.

"You were lucky."

Babette and Jeebrelle uttered a low, "Oooh," as Serafina whirled quickly and stalked for the male, jabbing him in the chest with a finger. "Fuck you. That was more than luck. You're just mad because I didn't need a man to protect me."

He grabbed her hand and pulled her close. "If you're a target for the Shaitan, then the next attack might be worse."

"Can it be worse than zombie monsters, dragons, and talking cats?"

"I'm feeling attacked here. And faint from hunger," Kitty interjected.

"Maybe we should leave Serafina and Israfil to talk. I saw a cheese shop on my way over," Jeebrelle mentioned.

New favorite servant.

Kitty leaped from Babette's arms to Jeebrelle, the horseman the humans nicknamed Pestilence. The only thing she might poison was Babette's heart. There could be trouble ahead for those two.

Not Kitty's problem.

She just wanted the cheese.

All the cheese.

A good start to a day that she predicted would end tragically if she didn't eat soon.

Chapter Fourteen

The cat departed with the two women, leaving only Israfil, who still held her hand. Serafina yanked it free.

"You should go with them."

"I'm not leaving you alone."

"I didn't ask you to stay."

His lips pressed into a thin line. "I'm aware. However, it is my fault you were attacked."

"How do you figure that?"

"The *ubukka qabri* is a tool of the Shaitan. My enemy."

She rolled her eyes. "Sure, make this all about you. What a surprise."

"Why else would it have come here?"

"Did it ever occur to you that maybe it thought I was the threat? After all, you're not the only one hunting for the ring with the genie inside."

"But you don't intend to destroy it."

She arched a brow. "Why would I? Gotta say, I'm kind of thinking that would be a waste. Kitty did say if I freed the genie, I'd get three wishes."

His jaw dropped. "You can't release it. The Shaitan are dangerous."

"Says you. How do I know you're the good guy here?"

"Because—"

She interrupted. "Because you're arrogant and bossy? I already know that."

The thinning of lips expressed his ire. "The fate of the world depends on me destroying the Shaitan."

"You really are full of yourself. Here you are after being gone three thousand years, spouting off dire predictions. Meanwhile, the world has been getting along fine without you."

"You call the pollution and violence of this modern age fine?"

He would point out the biggest flaws in her argument. "Maybe I can wish for a cleaner planet or peace for all."

"Says someone who doesn't understand how it works. You cannot ask for something so vague and large. Wishes should be precise lest, they fail and sow even worse repercussions."

Interesting. "There's a limit on what genies can do?"

"Yes."

"Good to know. Now if you'll excuse me, I am done wearing rotted guts." She entered the bathroom and slammed the door shut. Leaned against it for a moment. Let out a deep breath. Then another.

In the commotion, it hadn't really hit her.

I fought a zombie.

A monster. Never mind her boast of having won. She shook as she realized just how badly things could have gone.

The hot water and soap sluiced the slime from her skin, but the tremor in her hands remained. She stood under the scorching spray until the room filled with so much steam she could barely see. Only then did she finally turn the water off and wrap herself in a towel.

Perhaps it was time to forget about the ring. Let Israfil find and destroy it. If hunting it brought zombies, what could she expect if she actually got her hands on it? Would one of those Shaitan attack her? She couldn't help but remember her dream, seeing it now in a different context. Had that been one of the genies talking to her?

It sounded crazy.

Crazier than what she'd experience thus far?

She'd forgotten to bring clothes with her and emerged in a towel, startled to realize Israfil stayed behind and appeared to have done some tidying, the scorched smell replaced by a flowery scent, her bed freshly made. The window, though, remained broken. Would the hotel believe her if she said a bird hit it?

"Why are you still here? I thought you'd be running off after your cat." She tried to act nonchalant, all too aware she wore only a skimpy towel. Heat flushed her skin as she remembered the last time they'd been alone together. Only hours ago, and yet it felt longer.

"Leaving did cross my mind, but I thought it best I stay."

"Because you don't think I can protect myself."

"No, you've proven you can. It's more…" He heaved a heavy sigh. "It didn't seem honorable not to include you in the search for the artifact after what you've already been through."

A chuckle escaped her. "I'm surprised you know that word." She bit her lip a second later as he recoiled in affront.

"A dragon mage is the most honorable thing there is."

At his reply, she snorted. "Honor isn't about power or rank but the morality displayed when faced with adversity."

He blinked at her. "If that were true, anyone could be noble."

Her lips quirked. "That's kind of the point.

Good actions reap rewards." She dug into her suitcase and found an outfit.

"Who defines good?" He waved a hand. "Don't answer."

"Why not? Or is this a case where human opinions don't matter?"

He frowned.

And she muttered, "That's what I thought." She slammed the bathroom door and dressed, annoyed at the man who thought so little of her species. Had he not noticed all that humanity had accomplished?

When she emerged, she found him by the open window.

"Still here?" she asked. She'd truly thought he'd have left after her latest goading.

"It will take more than a lively discussion and insults to chase me away."

"Shouldn't you be going after your precious artifact?"

"I am. Why do you think I waited for you?"

"Me? Why? You don't need me as a translator anymore. You have your friends to talk to Kitty." So much for being special and indispensable.

"I thought you wanted to locate the artifact."

Did she? Much as she wanted the money for the treasure, she really wondered if she'd live to collect it. Zombies crossed a line. What next? "I do want to find it, but what's the point? You've made it clear you're destroying it."

"Correction. I will kill the Shaitan within. At the same time, you asked before if I could do so without harming the vessel. That answer is yes."

Her spine straightened. "Meaning you'd get your genie and I'd get the ring."

He nodded.

It begged the question, "Why are you offering? Technically, you don't need me."

"I don't, and yet, I feel as if it's the right thing to do."

He truly seemed puzzled and rather than look a gift dragon in the mouth—and get possibly chomped—she asked, "Will there be more zombies?"

"Maybe. The appearance of one indicates a Shaitan in the area."

"Or a necromancer."

His turn to eye her blankly.

"Person who can raise the dead with magic."

He frowned. "Does that happen often?"

"Until I met a zombie, I didn't think it happened at all. Speaking of which, I'm still confused as to why that thing came after me."

"Perhaps it thought we found the ring."

Or it didn't want them acquiring it at all. "If this is about the ring, then since we're not giving up, we might be targeted again."

"I won't allow you to be harmed." A vehement declaration.

Earlier, his protectiveness roused her feminine annoyance. But now… "Are you offering to defend me against danger?"

"Maybe." He seemed discomfited at the idea.

"Why? Why do you care what happens to me? I thought I was *just* a human." She mocked him using his own words.

"You are. And I shouldn't care. But…I can't seem to help myself." He clamped his mouth shut and looked vastly uncomfortable.

"Thank you. It's sweet."

"I'm not sweet!" A hot exclamation.

"No, you're not. You're gruff. And arrogant. Often an ass. Yet, despite it all, you're a decent person."

He grimaced. "Fuck."

It was his disgust that had her laughing and leaning up on tiptoe to brush her lips on his cheek so she could whisper, "My hero."

Chapter Fifteen

Israfil had been a warrior a long time, fought hard, been injured, and he'd almost died numerous times. He'd been rewarded for it, but in all that time, no one had ever called him their hero.

A soldier. A general. A leader. A killer. All titles he'd worn. At the sight of him, dragonkind bowed their heads in respect, whereas humans ran screaming when they weren't trying to murder him.

He was the scourge of the desert. A horseman of the apocalypse. A dragon mage best suited for war.

And this human accused him of being a hero?

He wasn't sure how that made him feel. Good, proud, also angry and insulted. Emotions at odds.

It didn't help she'd kissed him. Lightly, sweetly. The scent of her swirled around him. Boiling his blood.

He wanted nothing more than to take those lips, seduce her, and show her his might until she trembled—and cried out his name in pleasure.

Did she care about the tumultuous emotions she'd evoked with her words and actions?

Nope. She moved away from him and began stuffing items into a bag. "Where did they take her majesty for breakfast?"

For a moment he thought she meant the dragon royalty. Then it hit him. "Kitty will want cream."

"Don't we all." She eyed him over her shoulder as she said it, and his cheeks heated.

A shocking reaction. He couldn't remember the last time that happened. Because it never had. He unsettled women, not the other way around.

With a wink, she sashayed out the door.

He almost dragged her back to see if she meant the kind of cream she implied. The very idea of her pleasuring him with her mouth…

It took a moment to compose himself before he followed. When he did, he moved quickly because if a Shaitan lurked, they might send more of their drones. The dead weren't their only tool. Bugs, found everywhere in the world, were a popular choice for a species that didn't have the numbers to form an army.

Israfil used the stairwell to descend and vaulted down the center of them, landing with bent knees and a slight thud. He startled two humans about to start the climb. He cast them an intense stare as he growled, "You saw nothing."

Rather than bow their heads or nod in acquiescence, the woman whispered, "It's War! I saw him on YouTube," and swooned.

The male barely caught her and quivered in fear. "Don't kill us, sir, er, my lord, um, please?" Spoken on a final, quavering note.

"That depends." He wouldn't, but Israfil appreciated that they recognized his greatness and properly reacted to his presence. He bared his teeth. "Tell no one I am here."

Israfil shoved through the door and entered the lobby in time to see Serafina passing through the glass revolving doors. Fool woman. Dawn had crested, but that didn't make the outside safe. Not all monsters attacked in shadows.

Annoyed, he stomped his way to the door.

A male dressed in a suit and very much human stepped into his path. "Israfil. It's been a long time."

Being recognized didn't surprise; however, his true name wasn't publicly known. He stared at the man. "I don't know you." The features were unfamiliar, the scent very human, and yet something told him to be wary.

"They are hurt." The male grabbed at his chest. "After all, thou were the one to personally stuff them in the prison."

The speech patterns identified the male as—

"Shaitan," he hissed. Only how was it possible? The Shaitan were beings of smoke, and the person in front of him remained most definitely human. "Have your kind started possessing people now?"

"Just a passenger and not for much longer. The soul in this body appears to have departed, and without the machines that sustained its life, the flesh is failing."

This took animation to another level, but of even more concern, it appeared another Shaitan had been released. How many did that leave? Was this the Shaitan from the catacombs they'd been seeking?

"What do you want? Why speak to me?" Because this was a departure from the past. In his time, the Shaitan brought strife without care, and the dragon mages did their utmost to counter it. Conversation never entered that equation.

A sibilant whisper. "They want to be free."

"Seems to me you already are." One by one, the containment objects were failing, releasing the Shaitan upon the world.

"They are not, and neither are thee."

Israfil arched a brow. "How do you figure I'm not?"

"Because thy primary goal is still hunting them."

"A worthy goal."

"Is it, though?"

The conversation had him frowning. "Of

course, it's worthy. The Shaitan are evil and bent on destruction."

"They have changed."

The very idea had him snorting. "I highly doubt that. Next you'll claim you no longer want to free the Iblis."

To his surprise, the male possessed by the Shaitan nodded. "They would prefer to keep the Iblis in its dimension. They don't want life to end on Earth. Without life, there is nothing."

A surprising reply. "Since when do you care?"

"Since they have lived three thousand years alone. It proved enlightening."

A possible argument, but Israfil had his doubts. "If you don't want to obliterate life, then what do the Shaitan want?"

"To live free. To not be hunted."

"You wouldn't be hunted if you didn't cause mass casualties," Israfil drawled.

"They will defend themselves if threatened."

"Is that what we're calling attacking these days? Barely released and already your kind have been back to their same old tricks, causing destruction everywhere you go."

"Only because they were divided at first."

Israfil snorted in disbelief. "And now you're not?"

"They who disagreed have died by thy weapon.

Now they who remain only desire freedom and peace."

"Says you. Pretty words that make you sound sincere and benign, but how can we trust you?" Because he didn't doubt for a moment the Shaitan lied. Death and destruction, that was their motto. Never mind the fact he'd met another who'd changed.

Daava, a former Shaitan, had emerged from her imprisonment as an individual instead of part of the Shaitan collective. She'd been ready to sacrifice her life to save Maalik, the dragon she loved. In return, Maalik used his last wish to keep her alive. But Daava was unique. She saw herself as a person, unlike the one he spoke to, who still seemed to be part of the hive mind.

"The humans have an expression: trust is earned." The possessed man offered a smile. "They would show their intent if offered a chance."

At the request he snorted. "Again, sounds great, but how can I believe you?"

"Have they attacked?" The man spread his hands.

"Not in this moment, and yet my companion was targeted recently."

The male grimaced. "An unfortunate misunderstanding."

"How is it a misunderstanding? You sent a zombie to kill a human."

"Not kill. Retrieve. They thought the human had found something. They were mistaken. It won't happen again."

"No, it won't, because I won't allow it. And you know I have the weapon to back my promise." The God Killer appeared in his hand, drawn from the dimensional pocket he kept it hidden in.

The Shaitan glanced at it. "They expected something grander."

"Doesn't need to be fancy to kill."

"The reminder they are susceptible to mortality does much to keep their base impulses in check."

"Does it?" He had his doubts. "I should eliminate you now and save myself the effort later."

"Killing this body will not eliminate them, as they are not actually here."

"It would shut you up, I'll bet."

"It would be a mistake because they have an important message. About the ring thou seek."

Israfil almost rolled his eyes. "Let me guess, you want me to free the Shaitan within instead of killing it."

The man shook his head. "On the contrary. Thou must ensure they die for they, above all others, would never rest until the Iblis is brought to this world."

An unexpected response. "What makes you think they haven't changed like you and the supposed others?"

"Because it has been seen. A future where they are set free. It doesn't end well for anyone. Not even them."

It might be the first time Israfil saw genuine despair in a Shaitan. Or had he never been willing to look before?

Maalik had fallen in love with Daava because he'd seen, in her, a redeeming value. Was killing them all the right answer? Could it be time their war finally ended?

"What's your name?" he asked suddenly.

"As they are the first to realize the new purpose, they have chosen Adevem."

He shook the Shaitan's hand and noticed their surprise. "Don't let the next time I see you be because I have to kill you, Adevem."

"They've seen that future. It ends badly for all." With a cant of his head, Adevem left, literally. The spirit inhabiting the body evaporated, and the shell left behind collapsed to the floor. Not that Israfil paid it any mind.

He headed for the glass door, wondering at the strangeness of the conversation. Could the Shaitan be believed? Or had this just been a distraction ploy to keep him away from Serafina?

Suddenly chilled, he raced to find her.

Chapter Sixteen

It wasn't hard to find the cat, as Babette and Jeebrelle had chosen to sit outside a bakery at a tiny bistro set cordoned off from the sidewalk. Kitty perched on a round, wrought iron seat with a padded cushion and lapped from a dish, pausing long enough only to say, "Did you fornicate yet?"

"No!" Serafina sputtered. "We did not. Ew."

"You should," Kitty declared. "Mating heat is clouding my servant's mind."

"Mating heat?" Babette purred, leaning forward. "Tell us more."

"Let's not because there is nothing between me and Israfil." Serafina chose to focus on the cat instead. "What happened to you claiming I was the only one who could hear you?" It miffed her that she now shared that ability with others.

"At the time, I meant the wish to be about you,

only I couldn't pronounce your name and, well, kind of forgot it given its lack of importance, so basically asked for the next females I came in contact with to understand me."

"Females in the plural?" Serafina asked, sitting in the chair left at the four-person table.

"Just in case the first one I came across proved too stupid."

"I guess now you're going to tell me my services are no longer needed." A depressing thought because, despite all the strangeness, Serafina couldn't deny enjoying herself.

Kitty uttered an unfeline-like snort. "You cannot quit. Serving a goddess is for life."

Israfil might be pompous, but somehow his cat surpassed him. "Um, you do realize I never agreed to be your servant?"

The cat proved undeterred. "No agreement necessary. You were chosen. You're welcome by the way. I realize what a great honor it is for you." Kitty raised her paw and licked it clean before then going in for the gold under her tail.

"I am not worshipping a butt-licking pet," Serafina muttered.

"Easier to just go along," Babette whispered. "My mom had this terror of a dachshund when I was little. It used to chew on my ankles something fierce. But if I didn't move, she tended to not break the skin. Unless she was mad. Or hungry. Which was most of the time."

"I am not having a pet dictate to me." Serafina rose from the table. This was where she got off the crazy train. Let these women deal with the talking cat, the monsters in the sewer, and Israfil.

She whirled to find a massive chest in her face. Israfil's heat and scent surrounded her. She glanced up, way up, and found him staring down.

"I was just leaving."

"Good. Time to locate the next seal." He glanced over Serafina to the cat. "Has Kitty mentioned a location yet?"

"Over there." The cat extended a leg in reply.

Israfil didn't react, so Babette snickered. "Your pussy is something special."

For some reason he glanced down at Serafina before replying, "Yes she is."

Kitty suddenly jumped from her seat, tail up, announcing, "Let us go, peasants."

This time, Jeebrelle held the bemused expression. "Have cats always been this arrogant?"

"You obviously haven't been subjected to any cat memes yet," Serafina muttered. "Probably the most popular one being, 'Dogs think they're human, cats think they're gods.'"

"Don't think, we are." Kitty sniffed.

As they set off following the light-stepping feline,

they must have seemed odd to those passing by. A flamboyant Babette was dressed in a pink velvet tracksuit with Juicy printed on the ass. Jeebrelle was in a jumpsuit of pale yellow belted with green that loosely framed her. Israfil, still wore his cloak, albeit with the hood down, and Serafina was the only tourist-looking one of the group with her sturdy hiking boots, jeans, sweater, and jacket, finished off with a backpack.

They walked for longer than she liked. Israfil dropped back to walk with Jeebrelle, whispering, heads bent together. A fact she knew because she glanced back more than once.

And got caught.

"You don't have to be jealous. They're like brother and sister, not to mention Jeebs and I are kind of a thing," Babette boasted.

"I'm not jealous." A lie. Serafina felt hot annoyance at their private conversation.

"Perfectly normal since you're his mate."

There was that word again. Serafina waved a hand. "Whoa with this mate stuff. One, I don't know what it means. Two, if it means what I think, then hell of a no. And three, he's not my type."

"You're into girls?"

"No!" It emerged a tad vehement, and so she hastened to explain. "I mean not that there's anything wrong with liking girls. It's more that he's not..." She trailed off as she realized she wasn't sure if Babette knew his secret.

"Not human? I know. I can see where that might cause you some concern. If it makes you feel better, I have a few friends who are mixed mates. As in dragon married to a human. Seem to be doing just fine. And in case you're worried, the plumbing works all the same."

"Er." She had no reply for that, so she added a weak, "He's much older than me."

"Jeebs is, too. Just means they're more experienced." Babette nudged her and grinned. "It's not a bad thing, actually. Being locked away for so long has made them horny like you wouldn't believe."

The implication brought heat to her cheeks. "We are not having sex."

"Why not? Are you waiting for marriage?"

"No."

"Already with someone?"

She shook her head.

"Then why wouldn't you want to have fun with that hunk? He's almost sexy enough to make me wish I wasn't a lesbian."

"Because." Which wasn't even an excuse. How to explain that while he exhilarated, he also frightened. There was something intense about Israfil. Alien at times.

The cat abruptly sat down. "We're here."

Serafina wasn't the only one to glance around. "Here where? Which shop has an entrance into the catacombs?" because they stood on a sidewalk with stores flanking both sides of the street.

Kitty extended a paw. "I can smell it coming from there." There being the storm drain under the sidewalk's curb.

Israfil crouched and looked closer. "I scent nothing."

"Tell my servant his doubt has been noted and will require extra petting later for forgiveness."

"I am not telling him that," Serafina muttered.

But Babette did, and for a few seconds, Israfil went cross-eyed. Then he growled. "Tell Kitty that her scenting it does us no good. The opening is too small for us to use."

Kitty didn't need translating. She sniffed and sauntered to the hole in question. "Not my fault he's too fat."

Jeebrelle slapped a hand over her mouth to stifle a giggle. Babette roared with laughter, leaving Israfil flummoxed.

There might have been some mirth as Serafina relayed the message. "Your cat says you need to lose weight."

"My cat is a brat," he huffed.

"Your cat is also gone." Babette crouched down for a look, not that she would see anything. Kitty had disappeared down into the hole.

"Fuck," he muttered.

"I wouldn't worry about it much. Given how

much she likes to eat, I doubt she'll be gone long."
An answer that earned Serafina a glare.

Babette jumped to her rescue. "Your woman is right. But in case she's not, we should see if we can access this area of the sewer. There must be a person-sized sewer grate somewhere." She grabbed Jeebrelle's hand. "Let's go check in the alley."

The two women slipped off, leaving her alone with the dragon mage, who glared at the sidewalk as if he would tunnel through it.

"Should we be looking, too?"

"Not sure how that helps us. Even if we found an entrance to the sewers, I cannot scent the arti-fact," he muttered with obvious disgruntlement.

"I'll admit I don't know much about the smelling thing, but couldn't you sniff out your cat?"

"Maybe. Kitty can be tricky to track at times."

"I might be able to help. I've got all kinds of maps of the catacombs and even parts of the sewer system stored in a cloud. I just need to get a new phone to access it." With that, she began walking, and he kept pace. Handy, as his size and his cloak kept people from crowding their path.

She found a store selling pay-as-you-go cell-phones and bought one that the clerk promised came fully charged. Outside, she swapped her SIM into it and smiled as she pulled up a schematic.

She pointed. "This is the layout for the sewers in this neighborhood."

"That doesn't help us much since Kitty will have found some kind of impossible route into the catacombs."

"Then we'll find one, too. The catacombs are famous for having all kinds of entrances. There must be one in this area." Chewing her lower lip, she glanced around, for what she couldn't have said. It wasn't as if an illegal entry point would be advertised.

"I know a way, but the humans won't like it." He glared at the sidewalk as if he'd laser it with his sight.

"Before you start destroying things, maybe we should ask someone if they know a way into the ossuary nearby."

"Ask who?" he scoffed.

A loud, "Pssst," had her glancing around then down to see a homeless man sitting slumped within a doorframe. "I know how you can get to the old tunnels."

"Tell me." Israfil loomed and did his best intimidation glare.

The vagrant held out his hand.

"Does he want me to bite it off?" Israfil growled.

"He's looking for money." She handed over a bill. The man tucked it away before saying, "There's a store selling sex toys two blocks that way." He pointed. "They've got a secret entrance in the back. Tell the clerk Gaston sent you."

"Thank you." She glanced at Israfil. "Shall we check it out? Or do you want to find your friends first?"

"They can find us when they're done."

She almost asked done with what then thought of how Jeebrelle's cheeks bloomed with color as Babette led her away. Must be nice to be lusty and in love.

For some reason she glanced at Israfil. Lusty for him? Totally. But she could never love someone like him. Just imagining made her wonder what it would be like to be the focus of his affection. Intense, she'd wager, not that she'd ever know. He'd made his stance on humans quite clear, although Babette might have a point about having sex with him. It might be worth the experience.

As they walked, she noticed him staring at people they passed, sometimes even glancing over his shoulder suspiciously.

"Is there a problem?"

"No," he said grumpily.

"Then why are you acting as if everyone around us is a potential enemy?"

"Because they are."

"Are you always this paranoid?"

He stiffened. "It is not paranoia to be cautious. The enemy has acquired new tricks."

"The enemy being the genies you're trying to find." She still had a hard time wrapping her head around it.

"I found one, actually."

Her next step halted midair. "When?"

"Before I found you and the others at that cafe."

It hit her with a bit of horror as she gasped, "It was in my hotel?"

He nodded grimly. "Yes. Waiting for me."

"What did it want?"

"It claims it's changed. That it wants to live freely and without harm."

A frown tugged her brows. "You don't believe it?"

"I think they would lie to save themselves."

Having never met one, she couldn't answer as to their truthfulness, but she did have a reply. "Is it possible that not all of them are evil?"

"No."

"Why?"

He whirled on her. "Because it is in their nature."

"It's in a lion's nature to hunt and kill, but even they will make friends with those they'd count as prey."

"And in that analogy, can you guarantee none of those prey they've supposedly befriended will ever come to harm?"

Thinking of the news stories she'd seen of

beloved pets turning on their owners, she shook her head.

"While I will grant it is possible one or more of the Shaitan have changed, the chaos and death they could cause if we're wrong would be unimaginable."

"Aren't they restricted in their actions by the wishes people make?"

"To a certain extent only. They've found ways around the rules that bind them. Rules that would cease to exist if someone wished them to be free."

"Wait, there are rules?"

"The Shaitan are bound by a contract that forces them to grant three boons to whomever frees them. Being greedy, people have always used those for themselves."

"But it's possible to free them?"

He nodded. "Mikhail freed one called Daava, only he didn't so much free her as make her into a dragon not bound by the contract."

"Do they have to change species to be unbound? "

He shrugged. "I don't know, and I'd rather not find out."

The reply had her chewing her lower lip. "I feel like there's much we don't understand."

"On that we are agreed."

She saw the sign for the sex shop before they'd

reached it and almost cringed at the thought of entering.

A bell rang, and a feminine voice said, "*Bonjour et bienvenue. Je peux vous aidez?*"

"*Non, merci,*" her hasty red-cheeked answer to the older woman behind the counter.

The woman's long, gray hair was almost to her waist. She had a slightly thick torso and wore a loose white blouse and bohemian-style skirt. She appeared rather ordinary compared to the wares in the shop.

Shelves of lubricants promised non-greasy fun or flavored pleasure. Racks of clothing boasted latex, leather, and lace. The wall displayed crops, flogs, and manacles. But the true shocker was the dildos laid out in all their engorged, ridged, and—in some cases—odd combinations, like the one with numerous tentacles or the narrow version with the very bulbous head. Embarrassing to a woman who didn't own any sex toys but apparently it was even worse for a man who'd been locked away for three thousand years.

He roared, "What perversion is this?"

Chapter Seventeen

I srafil was by no means a prude or a virgin, nor an innocent when it came to sex and its accoutrements. However, the realistic penile statues and the completely fabricated kind crossed a line even for him.

Serafina put her hand on his arm. "Calm down."

"I will not be calm. This is not okay." His hand swept to a large box titled The Dragon Cock. It most certainly wasn't. The only thing it got right was size. The rest of it, from the wings at the base to the snouted tip, was completely wrong.

"It's okay," Serafina muttered. "Remember, we're not here to buy anything."

"Can I help you?" the woman behind the counter asked in a heavy accent. She eyed Israfil up and down in a way Serafina didn't appreciate.

Before he could blast her, Serafina said, "Gaston sent us."

"Oh." That raised a brow. "You're tourists?"

"Yes. We're interested in the catacombs. Can you help us?"

"But of course. Of course. " The woman emerged from behind the counter. "Follow me, *s'il vous plait.*"

With no qualms at all, Israfil shadowed the clerk, but Serafina paused with a frown.

Israfil glanced at her over his shoulder and arched a brow. "What's wrong?" He dropped back to her side.

"It seems too easy."

"It does." On that he didn't argue.

"Shouldn't she have demanded payment? Gaston was quick to ask, and yet this woman, no question. No request. It feels wrong." Serafina frowned.

"Perhaps she is waiting to show us the doorway first?"

"Or she sees us as tourists who are easy marks for robbery. I've heard of crime rings that target out-of-towners."

"Me, easy?" He snorted.

"I'm glad you're not worried, Mr. I'm A Powerful Dragon Mage," she said sourly.

"Neither should you be. I will protect you."

Before she could reply, the clerk shouted, "Are you coming or not?"

"We are," he said loudly.

Serafina mouthed, *Be careful.*

A single brow arched as he grinned. Not a comforting kind of smile. More the kind that said he'd like to see anyone try anything. She tucked close, trusting in him as she should. After all, Israfil didn't get his reputation as a fierce opponent by being nice.

The back room proved less jarring than the front, with metal shelving holding boxes. The clerk led them through to a small door practically hidden between two standing units.

The female waved. "There's the entrance you're looking for."

"You're not charging us admission?" Serafina remained uneasy by the transaction.

"If you're here, then you already paid Gaston. My job is just to give access."

"To anyone who asks? What if we were law enforcement?" Serafina insisted.

"Why are you assuming there's something illegal about it?" The clerk flicked her hair. "Use the door or don't. *Je m'en fous.*"

The female moved back to the front, and Serafina eyed Israfil. "What do you think?

"I think she is lying about something."

"You don't seem worried."

"Because I'm not. Any trap below was meant for humans."

"I'm human," Serafina reminded.

"Under my protection," he grumbled. "Or do you doubt my ability to keep you safe?"

"I can keep myself safe, thank you." Indeed, she'd proven that with the undead thing. "Nothing to be scared of," she muttered.

When she took a deep breath and would have pushed past him, he halted her. "I'll go first."

Rather than argue, she nodded. "Go right ahead. I'll be behind you with my backup can of pepper spray." She dug a can from her knapsack as he opened the door. Her alarm proved contagious. A hidden place without locks? It began to feel more and more like a trap.

The door opened onto a small room with a hatch in the floor, currently wide open. A dank square emitted a stringent scent.

He wrinkled his nose as Serafina muttered, "I smell bleach."

"Which is?"

"A way to clean up things that might be troublesome if someone were to investigate."

As he put a foot on the ladder, she whispered, "Be careful."

His cocky reply? "Never."

Chapter Eighteen

R ather than descend the ladder, Israfil dropped down the hole, hitting with a slight thud. He glanced up. "There's no one here."

"Do I need a flashlight?"

He shook his head. "There is light." He held up his arms. "Jump. I'll catch you."

"I'm capable of climbing down a ladder," she grumbled as she began her descent.

The tunnel below, built with rocks and brick mortared together, most of it old, but showing signs of recent patching, appeared empty in both directions. The light, a simple wire strung with a total of three bulbs, only extended about a dozen feet on each side.

Nothing untoward to see and yet the hair on her neck lifted. "This is going to sound dumb, but this place gives me the creeps like the ossuary didn't."

"I sense nothing."

"Because your senses are never wrong?" She couldn't help the sour sarcasm.

He opened his mouth and shut it. "Actually, my senses are somewhat dulled, so it's possible there is something down here with us, but again, you've nothing to fear."

"Never said I was scared."

"Then why do you tremble?" He reached out to stroke her cheek.

Explaining being close to him did strange things to her wasn't happening. "Just chilly."

He had a solution for that. He drew her close, the heat of him more than just that of the closeness of his body. "It is not that cold."

She glanced up, eyeing his mouth. She really should stop thinking of that kiss. His touch…

"You need to stop," he rumbled.

"Stop what?" she asked.

"Now is not time the time to distract me with your feminine wiles."

She arched a brow. "Seriously? I haven't done anything."

"That's the problem. You don't need to," he complained.

Which she took as a compliment.

He moved away, and the acute loss hit her. Rather than become one of those clingy women she hated, she gave a cursory glance in both directions and said, "Which way?"

"Choose a direction."

They went left first, only to quickly turn around as they hit a dead end. The solid stone appeared old and seamless and reeked of cleanser, as if someone had poured it out.

"Guess we're going the other way," she quipped. They passed the hatch and followed the tunnel past the last bulb. Once her eyes adjusted, the gloom beyond it revealed a junction with both side tunnels blocked by thick metal gates.

He grabbed the bars and rattled them.

"Want me to pick the locks?" she offered.

Before he could reply, the distinctive clang of the hatch closing had them both looking back in the direction they came.

"That bitch! She locked us in!" Serafina exclaimed, huffing hotly in her panic.

"Bah. We're fine. That puny hatch can't stand against a dragon."

His lack of worry eased her somewhat, until the lights went out.

Chapter Nineteen

The lights went out, and Serafina clutched Israfil, but not in passion.

"That can't be good," she muttered.

"I wouldn't say that. Decadent things can be done in the dark." Then again, if she were involved, he'd rather see every expression and the flush on her skin.

"Not exactly the time for that," she muttered, and yet her pulse quickened. "I have a flashlight in my bag. Hold on. I'll grab it."

He heard her rummaging and opted for a faster solution. The ball of light, conjured via magic, hovered mid chest and offered faint illumination. The stone lining these walls must have some of the same properties as the other section of catacomb muffling his abilities. Annoying, yet she appeared impressed.

"That's handy." Serafina blinked at him as she clutched her flashlight.

"It's nothing." Literally. The things he could do… Wouldn't work in this small underground space.

"Is it locked do you think?" She aimed her beam upwards at the closed hatch.

He flicked his fingers at it, giving it a magical push. It didn't budge and appeared to repel his efforts, causing him to frown. He knew of only one element capable of rebuffing a dragon. Dracinore. He eyed the walls in a new light. Traces of the rare metal would explain his weakness.

"How are we going to get out?" She shone her beam around. "I wonder if we can find an exit past those gates."

"No need. Stand back while I handle the situation." His shoulders were firm enough to be used as a battering ram. Once he busted them out, he'd have a chat with the clerk.

Rather than move away, she glanced back down the dark tunnel they'd just traversed. "Did you hear that?"

He almost scoffed. As if her human ears would have caught something his didn't.

Clank. The creak of a door opening on rusty hinges couldn't be missed.

They weren't alone. Sniffing revealed nothing. The cleansers used masked whoever approached.

"Who's there?" she stupidly huffed, aiming her flashlight down the tunnel. The beam did little to penetrate the shadows.

In the silence that followed came the clear scrape of something dragging over the stone floor.

What approached? Nothing good he'd wager, given how his whole body prickled in warning. A fetid stench managed to overwhelm the bleach, and the recognition of it had him tucking Serafina behind him.

"What is it?" she asked in a whisper that might as well have been a shout. Not that it mattered. Whoever shared this space with them already knew of their presence.

"Trouble." But nothing he couldn't handle. It might have been three thousand years since he'd fought a ghoul, but they weren't that difficult to defeat. Mindless beings, whose only thought revolved around hunger—a hunger fed by flesh and blood. "Stay here while I handle it."

"Handle what?" she squeaked. "And what's that smell? It smells like something died."

"Because something did," he said. He doubted she'd ever encountered a ghoul before; therefore he stuck to something she might understand. "There's a monster ahead."

He strode toward the threat, the mage light bobbing ahead of him. It caught the dull gaze of the ghoul, a milky film over its eyes showing its blindness. Not that it affected their ability to hunt, as they detected life force. Its gray skin, mottled and wrinkled, indicated its age—a few years at least. Most never lasted long. The lips had drawn back from the teeth, jagged black stumps in spots, filed points for others. It breathed, and what it exhaled invoked memories of decayed bodies.

Disgusting creatures. An example of what happened when the vampiric virus failed to take in a human host. He'd be doing it a favor putting it out of its misery.

It lurched toward him, dragging a crooked foot. Israfil stood his ground and waited. The ghoul reached for him, and he easily dodged, slapping aside the flabby arms while, at the same time, grabbing it by the neck.

Snap. With a twist, and with a heave that had him grunting, he decapitated the ghoul by brute force, increasing the putrid smell in the tunnel. The inert body hit the floor, and he tossed the head down the hall. Ideally, he'd like to burn it, even as he knew that corpse wouldn't rise again.

The head rolled back as if something kicked it.

He eyed it then the hall it came from. He sent the globe of mage light away from him, illuminating the tunnel and almost cursed as he realized the ghoul didn't hunt alone.

More of them crowded the corridor, shuffling in his direction.

The sight of so many had him issuing a warning to Serafina. "Move back and don't get close to them." They would rip her to shreds if given the opportunity.

She didn't argue, and he sensed more than saw her retreating down the tunnel they'd briefly explored that ended in a dead end. With her out of the way, it left him more space to move—and become the killer that earned him the nickname War.

He bared his teeth at the mindless ghouls and growled, "Die, filthy creatures." As if they understood the challenge, they surged, dirty claws reaching for him, teeth snapping for a bite. They might have the numbers, but he had the cunning and experience.

He tore into them, quite literally. Gripping arms and tearing when possible. Using a severed limb to slap gnashing teeth. He punched. Shoved. Slammed against the wall and crushed the one that tried to grab him from behind.

He acquitted himself well, but even he had limits, and the wave appeared never ending. Just how many were there? It didn't help the tunnels sapped his strength and he couldn't shift in the small space. His dragon would have made short work of these lesser creatures.

Still, Israfil never gave up. He fought and snarled as a group of them piled on, a distraction that some used to sneak around him, going for easier prey.

Serafina.

"Like fuck!" He whirled and roared, and while he wasn't a dragon to blow fire, his magic, even if weak, could ignite.

The flames were a pale orange as they licked the scraps of garments. The smoke and stench watered the eyes, and he heard Serafina coughing in the distance. Dammit, he'd forgotten about her more fragile human constitution. He extinguished the flames and drew the smoke away from her end of the tunnel.

The ghouls suddenly stilled, and a chill filled him. He whirled to face the vampire who must have made the ghouls. She stood a few paces away. Calm. Beautiful. They always were. It was how they fooled people into baring their necks.

Her lips curved into a smile. "Well. Well. If it isn't a dragon. It's been a while since I've seen your kind setting foot in my domain."

He scowled at the woman with the luxurious hair. "Apparently you've forgotten we shouldn't be trifled with. Call off your pets." Because while they'd mostly frozen at her appearance, the one at his feet licked his ankle.

She snapped her fingers, and the ghouls shifted to give him room. "Don't blame them for their eagerness. After all, your kind is so tasty and hardy.

Why the last dragon we had lasted several months."

A deep growl rumbled from within. "Are you trying to make me kill you?" Unlike ghouls, vampires could be more difficult to get rid of because they were sturdier and healed rather quickly. They could also mesmerize the weak-minded so that they stood still while they died.

She cocked her head and smiled, sending a thrill through him that had to do with a vampire's power of persuasion rather than actual liking. The fact he'd felt anything at all indicated her great age.

"You're feisty. And I'm bored. The other dragons in the city never come down to play anymore. I'd go up to the surface, but with the advent of electricity, there's too much light." She grimaced and still managed to appear perfect.

While not a man who usually bargained, knowing he had Serafina to protect, he tried polite-ness. "I didn't realize I intruded on your home."

"Hardly an intrusion. My servants on the surface have instructions to bring me people to play with."

"I am not a toy."

"All creatures are playthings so long as you have the right tool to keep them in check."

"There is nothing powerful enough to control me," he boasted.

"Isn't there?" Her smirk should have been his warning.

In the distance, he heard a scream.

He whirled. "Serafina!" Before he could lunge in her direction, cold metal snapped around his wrist. He'd made the mistake of forgetting how fast the older vampires could move.

A grab at the thick metal ring bracketing his flesh caused him to hiss. Magic kept him from ripping it off. "What is this?"

"A mixture of sorcery and dracinore. Do you like it? It's quite old and valuable because of its innate power."

He couldn't help but ask, "What does it do?"

"For one, it cannot be removed by the wearer. So don't bother tying. You'll just cause yourself pain. And secondly, it gives me control of you."

"Take it off," he huffed, trying to not panic. He'd gravely miscalculated. Worse, he'd failed Serafina. Not that he had time to care. When the vampire commanded him to, "Sleep," he could only obey.

Chapter Twenty

Serafina woke naked in a cage. Like literally. The cold metal bars and surrounded her on all sides. It hung suspended above a brackish pool of water illuminated by hurricane lanterns set around a chamber with crumbling brick walls dotted with broken stone pillars. An old place by the looks of it, empty of people.

The last she'd seen of Israfil was when he sent her to safety while he fought the monsters. She'd not argued because, honestly, she had limits when it came to fighting. So much for his boasting. Whatever came after them in the tunnels must have been bad to take a dragon down—which didn't bode well for her.

Last she recalled, she was pressed against the stone wall at the far end of the tunnel, listening to the hissing and grunting and thudding as Israfil fought whatever attacked, which turned out to be something humanoid, and frightening. She'd held her can of pepper spray ready as one made it past Israfil and bared teeth in her direction.

The grayness of its skin and its milky eyes had her trembling in fear. Not quite a zombie, but pretty fucking close! And her without a lamp to bash it in the head.

Distracted by the monster in front of her, she paid no mind to the solid wall at her back. Not so solid, as it suddenly shifted and she tumbled into a secondary group of the monsters. They hit her in the head, and she passed out, waking in this awful place.

On the one hand, yay, she woke up and appeared to not have been nibbled on. At the same time, though, she doubted they'd put her in a cage for shits and giggles.

If Serafina made it out of here alive, she'd have a few things to say—and slaps to give—to the clerk who'd locked them down here. Plus, it might be time to invest in a machete. A sharp one and a gun with lots of bullets. Maybe even a flamethrower to be on the safe side.

If she lived being the key. Her current situation didn't present a positive outlook. *Deadly with a chance of torture.*

She clung to the bars and peered out, thinking herself alone until what she'd thought were piles of debris along the edge of the water moved, rising as if waking from a nap. The monsters had congregated in this massive chamber hewn in the very stone itself, damp, musty, and smelly. Blame the bones littering the ground.

She didn't throw up until she saw a human skull amongst them.

When the retching finished, she wiped a trembling hand over her mouth. There had to be a way out. Out of this cage. Then past the monsters. Through the tunnels. Up the blocked hatch.

The more she thought of it, the more despair clung to her. Insurmountable odds. But was she really going to give up?

First thing first. What could she do? They'd taken all her things: clothing, shoes, even the elastic holding her hair. If only she'd thought to tuck her lockpicks into her prison pocket instead of her bag. Then again, she could be forgiven for not expecting to be lured into a trap that would see her kidnapped and caged.

A commotion drew her attention across the body of water to a far wall that had a dark opening within it flanked by two braziers, which lit as if a switch turned them on. The ragged bodies on the ground rose and swayed, their low moans pimpling the skin on her body.

A woman entered, gorgeous with her lustrous long dark hair, smooth skin, and brilliant, pure black eyes. Even baring her fangs in a smile didn't take away from her beauty. She wore a long, slim-fitting gown of dark blue set with glinting rhinestones more suited for an evening of fine dining and dancing or even cabaret singing than a dank cave.

The beautiful stranger stood by the edge of the water and smiled at Serafina. "Hello, human."

Now there was a way to start a chilling conversation. "Who are you?"

"Some call me the queen of the night, or as the French prefer, La Belle Morte."

A beautiful death. Yup, still chilling. "What do you want with me? What have you done with Israfil?"

"Ah, your dragon lover. A fine male. Strong, too. I worried the bracelet might not hold him."

What was this lady talking about? "Where is he? Let me out." Two demands and they earned trilling laughter.

"Why would I set you free when you're about to be the entertainment? Nothing better than hearing the screams and begging as your lover betrays you, and the cries of recrimination after as the lover realizes what they've done."

It didn't take a genius to grasp her intent. "Israfil won't kill me." Or so she hoped. She had no idea what the man would do. As for the dragon…

The queen clapped her hands. "Ah, such faith,

soon to be dashed. Delicious. Just like your lover."
The woman licked her lips.

"What have you done to him?"

"How about I show you?" The wink only made
Serafina's foreboding worse. La Belle snapped her
fingers.

Thump. Thump. The thud of footsteps preceded
the arrival of the dragon, a massive beast she recognized. How could she not. Israfil was the only one
she'd ever met. His horns curved just as wickedly as
before. His scales refracted light despite their dark
sheen. But his eyes...they were pure black orbs
without the silver fire of before.

The woman cackled. "As requested, your lover
and my new favorite meal. I've not eaten so well in
ages."

"You horrible woman!" Serafina couldn't help
but exclaim, drawing his dark gaze.

"A woman needs to eat if she wants to stay
young." La Belle flicked her hair. "And I plan to eat
from him for a long while. This time, I won't make
the mistake of sharing with my greedy pets. Their
saliva tends to ruin the blood."

"Leave him alone."

"Or what? You're not in a position to make
demands, human. As a matter of fact, you won't be
alive for long. Since I couldn't be sure of my new
pet's compliance, I was keeping you alive in case he
needed incentive, but he's been a good boy, haven't

you?" The vampire reached out to pat his snout, and the dragon visibly shuddered.

"You won't get away with this."

"Oh? How do you figure?" La Belle teased. "There will be no rescue, human."

"Israfil—"

"Is controlled by me. He won't lift a claw to save you when my pets tear you apart. It's amazing how easy it is to get dragons to revert to their most primal nature. Simple-minded creatures who—"

The woman might have kept talking if Israfil hadn't suddenly bitten her in half and then chewed.

It caused quite a bit of consternation amongst the ragged humanoids. They rushed the dragon, who proceeded to destroy them, quite literally. She could only watch in in horror, hand over her mouth, as he decimated everyone in the room. He didn't stop until every twitching limb stilled.

What would he do next? She didn't dare breathe. It didn't matter. His gaze turned on Serafina. There was nothing of the man in it, and yet she still whispered his name.

"Israfil?"

He huffed, hot steam that poured from his massive nostrils. He splashed through the water to reach her, tall enough to look right into the hanging cage.

She now understood how a bunny felt before a

predator. Small. Weak. Facing certain devouring death.

Hold on. Was she just going to let herself be eaten?

She returned to the bars closest to him and grabbed them as she said, "Israfil. Are you in there?" Dumb question. But what else to say?

He blew on her, a hot, dry wind smelling faintly of anise. He nudged the cage, and it swung, bringing a shriek as she clung to the bars rather than get flung about.

The swaying of her prison steadied as he gripped it. She noticed the ring around his front leg. The bracelet the woman had spoken of. Could it be what caused him to act more monster than man?

His clawed grip squeezed the bars, and metal squealed. The atrocious sound made her want to cover her ears; instead she put her hands on the bracelet, cold to the touch.

The dragon froze before he brought his face close, one dark orb staring.

"What do you say we take this off?" she asked softly, her hands palpating it for seams.

He rumbled, part growl, part who the fuck knew. What she did know? There was a man trapped inside the beast. And that man was who she spoke to as she sought to find a way out for them both, the metal binding seamless on her first exam-ination.

"Grrr."

"That better be a growl of, 'Hey sexy, you look good in a cage,' and not, 'Hey, I'm going to eat you because I'm a dumbass who thought I could handle everything.'" She tried not to piss her big girl panties as he kept making an ominous noise. "Don't you sass me, Israfil. I'm trying to help."

The glare indicated he might understand a bit more than expected.

She offered a bright smile at odds with her racing heart. "Don't be mad at me because you met something bigger and badder than you. Then again, I guess you were the baddest since she's gone now."

Her fingers found a tiny latch. *Click.* The bracelet around his leg shrank as it dropped and hit the water with a splash.

The darkness in his eyes faded, but the glare remained.

The voice in her head, though? That was new.

Nothing is badder than me.

As if to prove it, he wrenched apart the bars. Thankfully dragons didn't have short T-Rex arms. She tried not to scream as he plucked her from the cage. He sloshed through the brackish water and set her on the ground rather than popping her into his mouth for a tasty snack. Still, he loomed, and she couldn't help but recall how he'd chomped the woman.

She shook a finger at him. "Don't you dare think of eating me."

He shifted back to his normal size, which remained tall and intimidating. Also naked. He eyed her up and down before he drawled, "I will eat you if I want, and you will enjoy it."

Chapter Twenty-One

Despite the situation, heat bloomed in Serafina's cheeks at his statement. "Not exactly the time or place." She tried to keep her gaze on his face rather than his impressive abs.

He glanced around as he muttered, "I'm aware."

"You mean you're aware now. Thank goodness. I'll probably have nightmares about how you got rid of that awful lady."

A grimace crossed his face. "That was admittedly unpleasant."

"No shit." And then because he'd been so arrogant, she couldn't help but tease. "What happened to a dragon mage being able to handle anything?"

"You would point that out." He grimaced. "My poor excuse is I was taken by surprise. I didn't expect her to have an enchanted bracer."

"Enchanted as in she could use the bracelet to control you?"

"Somewhat. Unfortunately for her, my willpower was stronger."

Good thing because the consequences otherwise would have been fatal for Serafina.

"What was she?" she asked, even as she had her suspicions.

"Vampire, and those other creatures were her ghoul servants."

Her eyes widened. "Seriously?"

"Do I appear as if I'm amused?" No, he seemed angry. "The nerve of someone of her ilk, thinking she can control a dragon mage."

"Guess you showed her, hunh."

"I'll need strong alcohol to wash the taste out of my mouth." His rueful reply brought an unexpected and inappropriate giggle.

"Do you often eat your enemies?"

"Only if they're especially deserving."

"I noticed you didn't munch on the ghouls."

No mistaking the distaste on his face as he said, "Do you eat rotten meat?"

That had her stomach roiling, and she almost gagged. "Point taken."

He stood back and eyed her with clinical assessment. "You are unharmed?"

"I'm fine." She couldn't help but inhale at the sight of that wide chest tapering down to—She averted her gaze. "What happened to your clothes? Last time you went from dragon to guy you kept them."

"They stripped me while I was unconscious."

She waved her hands. "Can't you conjure up some new ones?"

"While I can preserve my garments during a shift, I cannot create them, and with the dulling of my powers in this place, I can't summon any."

"Pity." Because her nakedness could have used some cover. Then again, now that he'd been reassured she wasn't injured, his smoldering gaze kept her warm. She shivered, and he misunderstood.

"You are chilled." He dragged her close to him.

"I'm—" Hold on, was she going to argue given how nice it felt to be tucked to his heated torso? The situation still sucked, though. "We should be looking for a way out."

"At the very least exiting this chamber of horrors," he agreed. He took her hand. "This way."

She stepped carefully around the shards of bone on the ground because she really didn't want to try and explain to an emergency room nurse why she needed a tetanus shot for a ghoul-chewed-bone stab wound. She didn't entirely succeed in avoiding the sharpness and winced.

He growled and, without warning, swung her into his arms.

"What are you doing?" she exclaimed.

"My feet are tougher than yours."

"You know, some would say you have a misogynistic attitude. Just look at the way you treat women."

"Not women. Just you."

"Because I'm human."

"No. Because I don't want to see you in particular coming to any harm."

"Why me?" She couldn't help but ask.

His reply? "You're special."

Ridiculous how much that muttered statement warmed her through and through. "I'm glad you weren't killed."

His chuckle proved wry as he said, "It would have been ironic if I'd survived this long, only to be taken out by a vampire."

"Still can't believe they exist. Are all the monsters of legend real?"

"Depends on the legend. Some are based on the truth, others on fear and a lack of understanding."

His long stride took them from the cavern of death into a tunnel lit by a ball of magic. The walls were smooth and, while dirty, still showed faint carvings in the surface.

"What is this place?"

"By the looks of it, an old temple."

"For which religion?"

"Judging by the mixture of symbols, it's hosted more than one."

"Do dragons have a religion?"

That brought a grin that transformed his face. "We used to be the religion. In ancient times, we were revered as gods."

"I'm sure you hated that."

"I do miss the offerings of food," he said mournfully.

Now probably wasn't the best time to boast she made a mean roast beef dinner. As if he'd want her cooking for him. That would imply him sticking around after they escaped this mess.

The tunnel had many branches, some smooth and obviously chiseled with tools, others rough openings that stank. She couldn't have said why he chose some over others. He didn't place her back on her feet until they reached a massive metal door, carved all over without a handle or a lock.

"I do believe this is the exit," he announced.

"How do we open the door?" she asked, eyeing it and the smooth wall alongside.

"We can't." He put his hand on it and winced. "It's made of dracinore and has been enchanted shut. The entire place is veined with dracinore, which explains why I feel weak."

"Your version of Kryptonite I take it?"

"If you mean it is a dragon's bane, then yes."

Not the most reassuring thing to hear. "So how do we get out of here?"

"We wait."

"For how long?"

He shrugged. "One assumes Jeebrelle or Kitty will eventually get worried and come looking."

"How will they know where to find us?"

"Luck?"

She sighed. "Not a great answer."

"You are frightened," he stated.

"Gee, I wonder why. I'm trapped underground with no food or clothing and was almost eaten by you."

"Are you disappointed by the almost part?"

"What? Are you insane? As if I'd want you chomping on me," she huffed.

"Oh, I think you'd enjoy it." His brow arched, and he glanced down, making it clear what kind of eating he meant.

She blushed. "How can you even think about *that*? We almost died."

"Bah. I've faced worse."

"Well, I haven't, and I'm filthy," she sputtered.

"Then let's do something about it."

Before she could retort, he swept her back in his arms and took long steps back to the last junction in the tunnels.

"Where are you going?" she asked as he took a different branch.

"You'll see."

The tunnels in the section he chose proved cleaner than the other areas, lacking the putrid scent of ghouls. Spaced lamps hung on the walls provided a soft glow, and the air warmed.

"Where are we?"

"The former vampire queen's private quarters," he declared with a flourish as they stepped into a cavern that wouldn't have been out of place in an opulent castle.

Stone walls were decorated with brilliant tapestries. Carpets covered the smoothed stone floors. Braziers heated the air while incense perfumed it.

But it was the pair of kneeling people, heads bowed, that had her muttering, "Um, Israfil, we have company."

"Fear not," he replied, setting her by his side. He then puffed out his chest. "I am Israfil, the slayer of your queen and your new master."

The male lifted his head and eyed Israfil. Only then was his collar visible, as was the fine chain that kept him tethered. "My lord. How may I serve thee?"

"My female requires accoutrements. As do I. Food as well."

"I live to serve, my lord." The man scurried off, his chain rattling with him, leaving them with the woman.

She lifted her chin and Serafina was struck by her youth and beauty, envious of her full lips and hair that hung just low enough to cover breasts, which would have been visible through her diaphanous gown. "How may I serve you, my lord?" Then she made it clear how she'd prefer as her gaze dropped to his man parts.

Serafina found herself snapping, "Shouldn't you be helping your friend?"

"Of course, my lady." The woman followed the male, but Serafina still scowled.

Israfil snorted. "You have no reason to be jealous."

"I'm not jealous," she lied hotly.

"If you say so." A smug reply to go with his satisfied grin.

A grin he lost as the male returned with a robe and, without asking, draped it around Serafina's shoulders before dropping to his knees and grabbing her foot to place a slipper upon it.

Serafina almost objected. After all, she could put on her own footwear; however, she rather enjoyed Israfil's simmering annoyance. Jealousy could go two ways.

The female returned with a robe for Israfil, but rather than dress him in it, she pointed. "Perhaps my lord and lady would like to bathe first."

"We would."

Serafina shook her head. "No."

"You said you were dirty," Israfil pointed out.

"I am, but I am not going to relax in a tub being waited on hand and foot by these poor people."

"It is our pleasure to serve." The male bowed his head.

"I've failed you with my impertinence." The female dropped to her knees and bowed her head.

It made Serafina sick to her stomach. "Please, don't kneel. You're free now. Tell them, Israfil."

"Releasing them is not a good idea," he murmured.

"Maybe in your time slavery was acceptable, but this is not the Dark Ages. People have rights."

"If I must." He sighed. "You heard my lady. You have your freedom to do as you please. Although, I warn you, the entrance to this place is barred."

"We cannot leave." The man grabbed the chain and shrugged.

It took Israfil putting his hands on the collar for it to split open. It hit the ground in a clatter. A moment later, the one on the woman joined it. The pair stood with hands on their necks, wide-eyed and speechless.

Serafina smiled and clasped her hands. "Your life of terror is over. Soon, our friends will find us, and you'll be able to return to the real world."

"You truly killed the queen?" the female asked.

"She's not coming back."

Serafina didn't expect the knife the woman suddenly lunged with, but Israfil did. He caught her wrist and squeezed until she dropped it.

"What are you doing?" Serafina cried. "We freed you."

"You killed our mother, the queen. And now we'll kill you." The woman thrashed in Israfil's grip and hissed, showing a mouth full of fangs. While distracted by her, the male grabbed his loose chain and wrapped it around Israfil's neck in an attempt to choke him.

"No. Stop." Serafina's pleas fell on deaf ears as the vampires repaid their kindness by trying to kill.

"Look away," Israfil growled.

Serafina turned her head as Israfil did what had to be done. Necessity didn't mean she liked it.

"It's safe now," he announced.

She glanced at the limp bodies and closed her eyes as she swayed on her feet.

"Don't move," he growled. He left the room with the bodies, and when he returned, he said, "I told you releasing them wasn't a good idea."

"You could have mentioned they were vampires, too," she grumbled.

"As if you wouldn't have still demanded I free them."

He had a point. She sighed. "Are there more?"

He rolled his shoulders. "Maybe. But doubtful, as young vampires require frequent feeding and the queen didn't seem like the sharing type."

"If they were vampires, then what are the chances there's any food?"

"Honestly? Not good. They don't have the same nutritional requirements."

"Are we going to starve?"

"No."

"But you just said—"

"Bah," he interrupted. "Don't worry about it. Not yet. I'll handle it. In the meantime, your bath awaits."

The room didn't just hold random ornate furniture—including a massive bed—but a stone basin big enough for several people had steam rising from the milky surface.

She eyed it with some trepidation. "It's safe?"

"Yes." And to prove it, he got in the water first. There was a bench or seat of some kind under the surface, for he sat down, leaned his head back, and sighed.

It proved too much to resist.

She dropped in beside him, groaning in pleasure at the heat. "This is heavenly."

"It feels good, I'll grant. But you haven't seen real heaven yet."

She opened one eye to squint at him. "What could feel better than this?" She swirled the water with her hand.

He reached over and dragged her into his lap. "Are you demanding a demonstration?"

"Um." She had nothing to say as his hands positioned her to straddle his thighs. His hard cock, pinned between their bodies, throbbed against her lower belly.

The corner of his mouth lifted. "Speechless? How rare. And here I thought it would take kissing to achieve that."

"Are you calling me annoying?" A breathless reply.

"Never." His lips curved with humor. "What you are is remarkable."

"Oh." Again, nothing to say.

"Do you feel clean now?" he asked.

Her body had lost the icky feel of the cage; the dirty thoughts inside her mind, though, had her licking her lips.

"I'll take that as a yes, which means it's time to eat," he announced.

"But I thought there was no food."

"There isn't. That's not the kind of eating I'm speaking of." And with that, he lifted her to sit on the edge of the basin and nudged her knees apart.

Chapter Twenty-Two

Israfil had been patient long enough. From the moment he met Serafina her scent drove him to distraction. The sight of her body enflamed him. But it was her mind and personality that he found most spectacular of all. She wasn't impressed by his rank or his power. She teased. She questioned. She pushed. And she showed no fear even when he was at his most dangerous. Only she could reach the man inside the beast and break the enchantment holding him prisoner.

It was a miracle she lived, given the ghouls and their vampire mistress. When that controlling bracelet went on, he'd found his will subjugated. He became little more than a primal beast. And then he entered that cavern where Serafina's scent tickled.

Seeing her. Smelling her. It brought him

partially back to his senses. Protecting her became more important than the burning curse demanding his compliance. The needs of a mate trumped all other magic.

My mate.

Found after three thousand years and what a surprise. He'd been sure he'd be alone forever. And he'd almost lost her. Even worse, she'd been harmed. Terrified. Afraid of him even as she faced that fear to free him.

Time to show her that he only ever wanted to give her pleasure, not pain.

He knelt in the tub between her legs and could have roared his pleasure at how she parted them farther to accommodate him. No denying her arousal, from her slumberous gaze to the quickening of her pulse and the honey pooling within her nether lips.

He did feel it only fair to give her warning. "I will bring you pleasure no other can."

"Feeling pretty confident, are you?" she teased.

"You and I are fated to be together."

Her laughter emerged rich. "There's that arrogance I've come to expect."

"More like accepting the fact that resistance is futile. You and I are meant to be."

"Big words and yet no action."

He growled as he leaned close. "I'll show you

action." He blew the last against her vulva, and she gasped. Her nether regions quivered.

She'd do more than that by the time he was done.

He wrapped his arms around her thighs to angle her that he might nuzzle her. The dampness of her pubes tickled. He gave her a long lick, and she moaned. He lapped at her again, spreading her lips, tasting her sweet honey. He flicked her button with his tongue, back and forth, making it swell. As her ardor grew, her breathing shortened into pants. Her fingers clawed at the side of the tub. Her hips undulated against his mouth.

"Yes. Yes," she chanted.

And he kept licking. But he didn't let her come, not yet. It was too soon. He wanted to enjoy her longer. When she drew too close, he pulled back and she moaned in loss, only to squeal as he rose enough to latch his mouth onto a pert nipple.

She grabbed at his head as he sucked and teased the nub. His hands cupped her breasts, and he fondled them. Weighed them in his palm. Kneaded them. He pushed them together and rubbed his face between and wondered what she'd do if he slid his cock into that valley and let the tip peek at her lips.

Another time. Right now, he was greedy and selfish. He wanted to taste her and tease her. He flicked the tip of tongue against her nipple and grunted in satisfaction as her head fell back, exposing her throat.

She probably didn't realize the trust she showed in that moment. He kissed the smooth expanse and had to hold back from marking it. The bite was a thing done in the olden days. He wasn't sure how she'd react.

He returned to her breasts and licked her nubs, one then the other, teasing her as he slipped a hand between her legs to play with her swollen button. Her hips gyrated and pressed against his fingers. She cried out when he thrust his digits into her molten channel. She gripped him tight, and it was his turn to groan.

She squeezed even harder as he sucked at her breast, taking in a large mouthful. She uttered soft breathy sounds of pleasure, but it was when she panted, "I need you. Inside me," that he could no longer contain himself.

He pushed himself from the basin, and he meant to lift and carry her to bed. But she kissed him the moment he had her in his arms. Her legs wrapped around his waist, trapping his cock between them. Only for a moment. She wiggled and shifted until the tip of him pressed against the entrance of her sex. He could hold back no longer.

With his hands holding her by the buttocks, he plunged into her. The pleasure had him grunting and stilling. Throbbing, too.

She squirmed and asked, "Are you okay?"

Yes. No. It has been so long for one. But mostly he knew that his world had irrevocably changed. He'd found the one, and the realization had him determined to make sure this first time was unforgettable for her.

He started out by bouncing her slow. In. Out. But his greedy mate clung to him and began using her own body to slam him deeper. Harder. She panted into his mouth. She moaned. She tightened.

His fingers dug into her cheeks as he held on, straining and almost in pain as he held back, waiting for her to cry out as she climaxed. He managed to hold on until her sex squeezed him so hard he gasped.

And then he couldn't stop himself. He rammed in and out of her, drawing out her orgasm as his own crested.

With a bellow that shook stone, he spilled inside her. His body was rigid as he found his pleasure inside of her. An ecstasy unlike anything he'd ever experienced.

He gave her his seed, a first for him, and whispered, "I am yours."

Now and forever.

She hugged him tight in reply.

He carried her to the bed, where they collapsed in a tangle of limbs, sated for the moment. He had a feeling he'd never tire of her.

He couldn't tell how long they slept, only knew they weren't alone when Babette drawled, "Ha, lost my ass. Should have known you two were fucking around, literally."

The silver dragoness didn't come alone. Before Israfil could react, a certain feline perched on his chest and uttered a long yowl of discontent.

Chapter Twenty-Three

"**I**'m hungry." The feline complaint woke Serafina.

It was followed by Babette saying, "I'll bet the lovebirds worked up an appetite, too. Bow-chicka-wow-wow."

"Actually, I've satisfied my hunger." Israfil was smug. A very man thing to say.

Serafina wanted to die of embarrassment. Bad enough she'd been spooning with Israfil but he just had to brag about the fact they'd had sex. As if it weren't obvious given their naked butts in bed.

Cheeks hot, she hid under the covers, which led to Babette laughing and Kitty swatting at her head while hissing, "Take that, evil under-the-blanket dweller."

She popped back out to glare at the cat, who eyed her serenely before saying, "Oh, it's just you."

"Where is Jeebrelle?" Israfil asked.

Babette jerked her head in the direction of the entrance. "Keeping watch. Says this place has some bad vibes."

"A vampire was living here with her ghouls," Israfil explained.

"I take it by the 'was' she's no longer around?"

He smirked. "You would be correct."

"What about her minions?" Babette asked.

"Dead."

"All of them?"

He nodded.

Babette's lips turned down. "You couldn't have saved us a couple?"

"Not my fault it took you so long to arrive," he quipped.

Serafina shook her head. "What is wrong with you people?"

"Nothing. We're perfect. And easily bored. Do you know how long it's been since I've fought the forces of darkness?" Babette whined.

"A week?" Israfil's tone was dry.

"Exactly. Ages!" Babette exclaimed, throwing up her hands.

"Next time, we'll save you some of the enemy," Israfil promised.

"You'd better." The woman shook her finger as if chastising him.

Kitty interrupted. "Too much talking. I'm hungry! Dying. Wasting away."

The exaggeration led to Babette clapping her hands. "You heard our feline goddess. Get your lazy asses out of bed."

In a rare moment of sanity, Israfil stated, "I think Serafina would like privacy to get dressed."

Israfil guessed rightly.

"I'll go, but talk about ruining a lesbian's voyeuristic fun." Babette winked at Serafina before she left.

Kitty remained sitting on Israfil's chest, calmly licking a paw and swiping it over her fur.

"We've been rescued." Odd how Serafina wasn't as elated as expected. Blame the fact she'd have preferred a little more alone time with Israfil. Make that more sex. That man and the things he made her feel… She finally understood why some people couldn't get enough.

"I told you they'd come," he stated as if he'd never had a doubt.

Serafina went to sit up, only to have him drag her against him, startling Kitty who squawked. "Hey! Watch it you, giant lug."

Israfil didn't care he'd annoyed the cat as he snuggled Serafina. He nuzzled her nape, sending shivers down her spine.

"Shouldn't we be getting ready?" She tried to be responsible.

"They can wait." His reason poked at her behind.

"But—" She might have argued more, only he palmed her belly, and her breath caught. "Make it quick." Probably the most insane thing she'd ever told a guy.

Having sex while people waited on them…well, it made it hot. Intense. Climatic. He worked a finger against her clit while pushing into her from behind, striking that sweet spot inside that soon had her tightening.

She orgasmed so hard she couldn't see or breathe for a second. He thrust one last time and held still.

"That's a better way of waking up," he rumbled, kissing her bare shoulder.

"I agree, but if we don't get moving, they'll probably come barging in again." And there would be no hiding they'd made them wait while they had sex.

"I could kill them if you want," he offered.

A giggle escaped her. "Not necessary. After all, I really would like to get out of here. I am getting kind of hungry." How long since her last meal?

"Mmm. Are you doing that on purpose?" he growled, nipping her skin.

"What do you mean?"

"I know what I'd like to eat."

Oh, how he tempted. It didn't help her resolve

because she remembered how it felt. Nothing she'd ever experienced could compare. But did it mean anything?

Her noisy belly ruined the romantic moment.

"I think I've just been told," he said with a grudging sigh. "Let's get you fed."

This time he didn't drag her back to bed when she rolled from it. She stretched and saw him watching her. It made her smile naughty as she purposely bent and twisted for no real reason other than she enjoyed his ardent stare.

She spent a moment by a full basin of water, splashing the sweat and sex from her skin. He joined her and smartly brought towels he'd located.

Her hair was a mess, and she couldn't bring herself to use the vampire queen's brush, but she did grab an ornate clip and twisted it atop her head. The outfit she had to settle on wasn't her usual style. The jumpsuit glittered when she moved, and the halter style left her back bare. She wore it without undergarments and was very aware of that fact with each move she made. Her sensitive nipples hardened in protest at the fabric covering them. As for her pussy... Well, it seemed their quick morning bout wasn't enough to satisfy.

By the time she found something for her feet that wasn't stilettos, Kitty had rejoined them from wherever she'd wandered, still complaining. "About time. I am wasting away. And does anyone care?

No. This is the thanks I get for notifying the others that you required assistance."

"How did you know we needed help?" Serafina asked, reaching to scoop up the cat, who immediately purred at being cuddled.

"A goddess always knows. Especially since my servant is an idiot and you're not much better, given you're in love with him."

The reply had Serafina blinking. She might have replied she wasn't in love, only Israfil was right there, listening and scowling at the feline.

"What is Kitty saying now?"

"Nothing," she said.

"Nothing wouldn't have dropped your jaw," he remarked.

"Just Kitty being her usual demanding self." Spoken perhaps a little too brightly. "Let's go." She strode away before he could question her more. Because she really didn't want to say the L word out loud. Not yet. Maybe not ever. It was too soon. She barely knew the guy, and great sex didn't make a relationship. Right?

Right?

They exited the bedroom to find Jeebrelle and Babette waiting. Well, Babette waited; Jeebrelle ran her fingers over the glyphs in the wall.

"This is fascinating," Jeebrelle murmured without turning her head. "According to these markings, this subterranean complex used to house a Dragon Sept, a family of grays. Apparently, they immigrated from the desert to here but, with the winters being so cold, carved themselves a home underground."

"What happened to them?" Serafina asked.

"It doesn't say. But I imagine a tragedy befell."

"Like a vampire?" suggested Serafina.

"Possible, although I'm not sure how one vampire could have taken out several dragons at once."

"She might have had help," Israfil muttered.

"Must have been quite the aid if she caught you," Jeebrelle teased.

He grimaced. "Thanks for the reminder."

Kitty yowled. "Talk on the way to the surface. Starving!"

Serafina almost laughed. "Someone is getting impatient."

"For once, I'm in agreement. Let's get out of here." Only as they passed the now open door did he ask, "How did you get past the dracinore door and enchantment?"

Jeebrelle frowned. "We didn't. The portal was open when we arrived."

"How?" he sputtered. "It was sealed shut."

"I unlocked it," Kitty announced. "A task that should have been beneath my notice. I really need more practical-sized servants. To think, I had to go inside the wall myself to deal with the mechanism.

It tore a tuft of fur." Kitty cast an annoyed glance at her hindquarter with a missing patch.

While Babette relayed Kitty's message, Serafina soothed the feline. "Your gracious act deserves an extra-large serving of cream."

"And sardines. The oily kind. It will make my fur smell good for that Tom I met in the alley. Although, if he thinks I'm having his kittens..." Kitty tilted her chin.

"They would be adorable," Serafina cajoled.

"That goes without saying. But what of my figure?" Kitty complained.

"Wouldn't you like children to pass on your knowledge?" She kept talking to the cat, not realizing Israfil paid attention until he purred by her ear, "I wouldn't mind a few."

The suggestion startled her enough she stumbled. The cat leaped from her arms with an annoyed screech. "Clumsy girl."

Everyone chuckled.

Everyone except Serafina, who suddenly wondered what it would be like to be with this man for life.

Chapter Twenty-Four

Israfil couldn't believe he'd said it. Neither could Serafina given how she glanced at him. The confusion on her face entertained. He'd thrown her off kilter, which seemed only fair; after all, she'd thrown him for a loop since meeting her. It took a chance encounter with the right woman to realize he wanted more from life than just hunting Shaitan. After all, what was the point in making the world safe if he didn't have someone to make it safe for?

Although the fact he'd told her he wanted children proved a surprise mostly because it never occurred to him. Before his imprisonment, he'd had no interest. During his incarceration, he'd been unable to imagine it, and yet now... Now he wanted it. Girl. Boy. Didn't matter. He just wanted someone to teach. Protect. Love.

A family to call his own.

It almost horrified him how quickly it happened. Blame Serafina, a human who'd not only managed to get under his skin but squirmed her way into his heart. At least now he understood his companions who'd succumbed. To think he'd been mocking them. Now he'd be the butt of their jokes.

Let them tease. He'd punch them. Hard. It should be noted Israfil didn't tolerate disrespect, even the jovial kind.

Jeebrelle guarded the rear with him, and he slowed his step, letting Babette and Serafina get ahead enough they could speak in privacy.

"You seem happy," she remarked.

"I am."

"Because of her." No need to specify who.

"Yes."

"Have you told her yet she's your mate?" Jeebrelle questioned.

"No." Nor did he realize it would be so obvious.

"Are you going to?"

"Eventually. So much has happened so quickly she might need time." Time to understand dragons weren't like humans. When they met *the one*, they knew. They might fight it, but fate would have its way.

"I wish you happiness, Isra. After all that's happened, you deserve it."

Did he? Three thousand years didn't erase the things he'd done. War wasn't just something he'd waged against the Shaitan. But that was a long time ago. The world had changed, and so had he.

But what would Serafina think if she knew the crimes he'd committed against her kind?

The route from the subterranean complex to the upper level proved easy. Just follow the stench of ghoul. When they arrived at the stone wall that concealed the secret passage, he growled, "I can't believe I didn't realize this was a hidden doorway." Or that he'd been fooled by the antiseptic smell. That alone should have warned him something was amiss.

It was only as they reached the ladder that Serafina paused and turned to him with a frown. "Are you sure we should leave? What about the artifact?"

"Fuck the artifact." Right now, he didn't care. His search for it almost led to Serafina coming to serious harm.

"Are we even sure it's down here?" Babette asked. "Because while you two were having fun in your vampire love nest, Jeebrelle and I scoured the sewers in this area. Found two illegal clubs, a home-less man who wanted us as his concubines, and a crocodile."

Serafina blinked. "A crocodile in Paris?"

"Probably flushed as a baby. I might come back to find it when it gets bigger. I've always wanted some croc-skin boots."

"Isn't that barbaric? I mean crocodile are akin to dragons, aren't they?" Serafina asked.

Israfil kept a stoic face as Babette ogled her and Jeebrelle appeared appalled.

It was the latter who exclaimed, "That's like saying monkeys are just like humans."

Only Serafina wasn't insulted. "Exactly."

Before someone eviscerated his mate, Israfil stepped in. "I think we'll leave the artifact for another day. Weren't you hungry?"

She bit her lip. "Yes, but it occurs to me that we should have searched those tunnels. Especially given there was a lake of sorts down there. What if it was the one mentioned in my research?"

"Do you want to go back now?" he asked.

The cat uttered a plaintive meow and glanced up at the closed hatch.

Whatever the feline said brought a frown to Jeebrelle's face. "Kitty says we might as well eat since you're wasting your time down here. She says the thing we're looking for has been found."

He exploded. "By whom?"

Jeebrelle shrugged. "Says she'll tell you after she is fed."

He glared at his cat, who appeared unimpressed and yawned.

Having been with her long enough, he knew better than to try and bully her into changing her mind. "Guess we're getting some food." He eyed the sealed hatch. "I see we're not the only ones who were misled. That clerk has much to answer for."

"Wait, someone tricked you into coming down here?" Babette guffawed.

Her mirth grated. "Wasn't that how you ended up in these tunnels?"

Babette shook her head. "Kitty led us a different way."

"I can't believe a human trapped you." Jeebrelle didn't even try to hide her grin.

It brought a huge scowl. "I could have gotten out anytime I liked."

"So he claims," Babette coughed into her hand.

Annoyed at their amusement, he smashed through the hatch, literally splintering it. As he rose from the hole he'd created, the clerk who'd lured them entered the storage room holding a sword of all things.

"You shouldn't be here!" she yelled, waving it. "Get back in the hole."

"I don't think so," he muttered. He hauled himself out that he might advance on the woman. The idiot didn't retreat but rather swung.

He managed to dodge the clumsy attack and tore the sword from the clerk's grip. That widened her eyes, and she turned to bolt, only to trip over Kitty who'd decided the floor by the clerk's feet was a good spot to lie down. The woman fell and smacked her chin off the floor.

She rose to a sitting position, blubbering. "I was just following orders."

"Here's an order. Be a decent human being instead of a murdering accomplice." Serafina was the one to get in the clerk's face. "You knowingly sent people down there to die as food for a vampire! Who does that?"

"A loyal servant," was the hissed reply as the woman lunged with a dagger.

His reflexes proved faster. He snared her wrist, broke it, and then, without any remorse—because after all, she'd dared attack his mate—he snapped her neck.

He tossed the limp body down the hatch head-first because, as Babette claimed, "We should make it look like an accident."

As if he cared. He'd like to see human authorities try and arrest him.

They emerged onto the streets of Paris to see night had long fallen. Most shops were closed, and only restaurants and bars still showed signs of activity. Food proved easy and copious to find, especially once Babette produced a credit card.

They filled their stomachs, even the bottomless Kitty's. At Babette's yawn, Jeebrelle said, "We should rest. We can plan our next move in the morning."

"Rest where?" he asked.

"My hotel if that's okay. I'd like a change of

clothes." Serafina grimaced at her outfit. Probably not a good time to tell her he rather liked it.

They returned to Serafina's hotel, where Babette and Jeebrelle rented their own room on the same floor. An exhausted Serafina sighed as they entered her chilly room. Seeing the window with its missing glass reminded him of what happened.

"It's not safe here," he declared, too agitated by her lack of safety to truly enjoy her stripping and changing into something she called pajamas. A waste really given he'd soon have her naked.

"You want to change hotels?" Serafina's lip turned down. "Do we have to? It's late."

"Actually I want to go home." By home, he didn't mean the hovel he'd been using these past few months.

"Where is your home?" she asked.

"May I show you?" A man used to taking and commanding, he asked her permission. "I can transport us there quickly if you'll allow."

She nodded. "I'd love to see it."

The portal he sketched took them to a mountain, a cold one that had his woman shivering and his cat complaining from her arms. He encased them in a bubble of hot air as they stood before a massive stone façade covered in ice and snow. Behind it was the door to his home. Technically not his but his parents' and where he'd been raised.

As a young man, he'd never bothered setting up

his own household. Too busy waging war and hunting the enemy. Only now that he sought respite did he finally understand what his father used to say about having a nest to come home to. A place to feel safe. No one would ever find them here. Especially once he renewed the many wards guarding the place. They'd faded without someone to renew them.

He placed his hand on the boulder covering the entrance, and with a nudge of magic, it slid aside.

"You live inside a mountain?" Serafina asked as she followed him into the massive tunnel, big enough to accommodate a dragon.

"I spent most of my growing years here." Away from the dragon politics his parents eschewed. Their lack of interest didn't stop him from seeking his kind out when he got to a certain age.

"Did you have siblings?" Asked as she entered the hollowed-out cavern that lit as he flung magic to the far reaches. He ignited lanterns that sputtered, the ancient oil burning off the dusty layer coating the surface before settling into a steady glow.

"I had two sisters, but they're long gone now." Part of the reason why he'd not returned here upon his release from his prison. Why would he? Because then he'd have to face the fact his family were dead.

"I'm sorry." Her hand on his arm proved a potent reminder that he didn't have to be lonely.

Together, they could start a family. Fill this mountain with the voices of children. With love…

He froze as the word filled him. Odd how he had no problem finally admitting he'd found his mate, but love? That actually terrified him. Love meant caring and being vulnerable. Responsible. Was he even capable?

Serafina wandered the massive space, investigating, sneezing as she disturbed millennia of neglect. A layer of dust covered everything, and all things fabric had long disintegrated.

He grimaced. "Give me a moment to clean up."

"Hand me a broom and I'll help."

At her offer, he laughed. "No need for such a mundane method. Watch."

He snapped his fingers, more for visual effect than need. A maelstrom erupted that swirled and drew all the loose particles layering the furniture, some carved of stone and lacking the cushions, others made of wood, petrified by time. He thrust the dust cloud out of his home and, when done, turned to see her gaping.

"That was so cool. What else can you do?"

He showed her. The fountain on a far wall had long run dry and took some warming before the snow and ice melted and began trickling to fill the basin. When it overflowed, a sluice took it away. She ran her fingers through it and splashed some on her face. "Chilly but fresh."

Given he used to sleep in a hammock strung overhead, he had to improvise a bed for them. He portalled out and returned with a mattress then blankets and pillows taken from a shop. Blame Serafina for his sudden conscience that made him leave a ruby in return for payment. The treasure room he'd plucked it from overflowed with riches, meaning he could buy Serafina anything her heart desired.

She'd gaped at the sight of all the riches. "This is yours?"

"Yes." Inherited from his family. It made him wonder when his lineage died out, given how much of the treasure filled the chamber.

"Do you have any idea how much this is worth?"

He shrugged. "Don't really care. A dragon can always take what they need."

"Is that so?" she drawled. "And does that work in reverse?"

"What do you mean?"

"Well, for example, what if a human needed something from you?"

"Such as?" he asked even as he had a clue by the smile on her lips.

"For starters, it's still a bit chilly in here. I could use a hug."

"Only a hug? I know what will warm you up."

He took her in his arms and turned her shiver

of cold into a passionate tremble. He made love to her gently in the bed he'd just made. His touch was soft, his movements slow, and yet that didn't detract from the climax.

Afterwards, they cuddled, and she said softly, "This feels like a dream. One I never want to wake from."

"It's real," he assured.

"Is it? You don't understand. I don't do this kind of thing. I mean we've never even gone on a date. Hell, we've only just met and yet…" She hesitated.

So he said it for her. "Being together feels right."

She turned in his arms to face him. "Yes, but it's more than that. I'm comfortable with you, and I shouldn't be. I mean you're a dragon mage. A horseman of the apocalypse, and I'm just Serafina, a regular ol' human."

"Just?" he mocked. "You are an incredible woman who shows immense courage in the face of adversity. You are attractive. Intelligent—"

"Stupid." Her nose wrinkled. "I almost got killed being nice to those vampires."

"Because you are compassionate. There are many things about you that I admire."

"How about I add one more?" She winked at him before slipping under the covers. She showed him a new talent with her mouth and hands, driving him to the brink of madness and ending her oral skills with the ultimate pleasure.

And as she snuggled in his arms after, he couldn't help but murmur, "I love you." But she was already asleep.

The next morning, he stroked the hair from her cheek and kissed the spot behind her ear, waking her gently.

"Go away with those magic lips of yours. It's too early," she grumbled, burying her face in the pillow.

He chuckled. "Someone is a little tired."

"I've had a rough few days. Just ten more minutes," she begged.

"How about longer? Sleep while I fetch us breakfast."

"And coffee?"

"And coffee." He smiled as he dressed, readying himself to leave. Apparently, not alone. Kitty jumped onto his shoulder, a sign she planned to go with him.

His smile didn't last.

He teleported to a quiet spot behind a column and potted tree in the lobby of the hotel as it occurred to him that he should probably check on Jeebrelle and Babette. In a stroke of ill luck, he ran into Adevem the moment he stepped into view.

The Shaitan had possessed a new body, that of a thin, young male with a red puckered scar across his temple. Adevem confronted Israfil while he sat in one of the lounge chairs.

"Israfil, how fortuitous to find you."

He doubted luck had anything to do with it. His reply was less than polite. "What do you want?"

"They already discussed their desire for freedom. Don't tell me in thy old age, thou hast forgotten, or should they blame thy mate for a lack of blood to the brain?" The smug smile wasn't what gave him the chill but the fact the Shaitan knew about Serafina.

"Cease the verbal games. Why have you sought me out?"

"Thou found the ring."

"No."

The Shaitan actually managed a passable frown. "No? How can that be? Thou were in the catacombs. Thou confronted the vampire queen."

"And?" Israfil didn't show his surprise that the entity knew of his actions.

"Surely thou located it."

He shrugged. "I didn't have the time. I was occupied with other things."

"Thou lie. The scrying shows it gone. Thou or thy companions must have found it."

"What scrying? Why are you so intent on finding it?" He leaned forward.

Adevem smoothed his scowl into a more benign expression. "They have told thee their concern about freeing the one in the ring."

"And I told you, when I find it, I'll destroy the Shaitan inside."

Only a twitch, there and gone, betrayed Adevem's agitation. "They must be found and soon. There isn't much time."

"Time for what?"

"If thou don't have it, then thou waste their time. Who else was with thee?"

"How about none of your fucking business. What is this really about?"

Rather than reply, Adevem looked past him to a spot over Israfil's shoulder where a wandering Kitty had returned to perch.

"The one who released the first." Adevem bowed his head. "Many thanks."

"You know Kitty?" Israfil asked.

"She is the reason they are here."

"Meow."

The Shaitan cocked his head as if he listened to the cat. Then replied, "Thou cannot make demands. Thou hast gotten thy three wishes from they, whom thou rescued."

"Meow," Kitty argued.

Adevem shook his head. "The rules are the rules."

Israfil couldn't help his curiosity. "What is she asking for?"

"She desires for thee to understand her words."

He glanced at his cat. "Guess you should have wished better."

Kitty batted his nose in reply.

"Don't start or I'll shave you," he warned.

She rubbed against him and purred. Odd how she could flip from annoyed to loving in a moment.

When Israfil turned back, Adevem had disappeared. Good riddance. He still didn't know what to make of the Shaitan.

Not long after, he was joined by Jeebrelle and Babette, strolling along, looking mighty relaxed. Would he also wear the same sappy smile now that he'd found Serafina? He sure hoped not.

"I hope that scowl is because that gorgeous mate of yours came to her senses and kicked you out of her bed," Babette drawled.

His smile might have been smug as he stated, "She's still sleeping in it."

"No, she's not. We saw housekeeping in her room on our way down."

He waved off their concern. "She's not here. We spent the night at my home."

"You left her in that dirty hovel?" Jeebrelle made a moue of distaste.

"Not that home. The one I grew up in. It lacks a few modern amenities, but with a little work and magic, it will make a fine residence."

"For a dragon. You do realize she's human." Jeebrelle pointed out the flaw in his plan.

"I hadn't noticed," he said dryly.

"You obviously aren't thinking straight. I've been to your home," Jeebrelle reminded. "It's not accessible to humans. How is she supposed to leave?"

"I'll portal her out."

"Meaning she needs you. What if you don't return?"

He frowned. "Why wouldn't I return?"

"I think what my main squeeze is saying is you're a dumbass who basically imprisoned that lovely girl," Babette elucidated.

"It's not a prison," he defended.

Babette uttered a rude noise. "Wrong. She can't leave, ergo, yes, it is."

"You're saying I need to find us a different home."

"Different, yes, and with layers of protection."

"Security from humans." He nodded. "Yes. I can provide that."

"Not just humans. Maalik contacted me last night," Jeebrelle announced. "Claimed he was visited by a Shaitan. Apparently, one of them has figured out how to temporarily possess the weak minded."

For some reason a chill took him. "Did this Shaitan have a name?"

Jeebrelle offered him a sharp look. "As a matter of fact, yes. They called themselves Adevem. Some kind of spin on Adam and Eve from the human religious texts."

He rose from his seat. "I've met Adevem. Twice now."

"And you're just telling me this now?" Jeebrelle exclaimed.

"The second time happened just before your arrival."

"What did the genie want?" Babette asked.

"They asked about the ring. For some reason, they thought I had it."

"Do you?" Jeebrelle asked.

"No."

Jeebrelle frowned. "The Shaitan asked Maalik if he could see where the ring was."

"Did Maalik give an answer?"

"Not one the Shaitan liked. Maalik would have questioned more, but Daava returned home, shifted, and ate the shell it was riding."

"I wonder if Maalik is who Adevem meant when he said he scryed for the ring," he mused aloud.

"I'm surprised you didn't kill the genie. I thought Azrael loaned you the God Killer," Babette reminded.

"He did." It meant he had to admit the truth. "I didn't kill the Shaitan because they seemed different."

The claim arched Jeebrelle's brow. "You think they've changed?"

"Maybe?" He shrugged. "And in any case, it wouldn't have mattered. By possessing a human body, my understanding is they aren't actually present."

"That was what Maalik said, too." Jeebrelle nodded. "What should we do about this Adevem?"

He shrugged. "I don't know." A strange answer given it used to always be kill.

Kitty meowed.

"What did she say?" Israfil asked.

It was Babette who blurted out, "Kitty says the Shaitan is a liar."

He cast a sharp glance at the cat. "Why?"

"She won't explain other than to add he's dangerous."

Funny, because his gut warned the same thing. "Maybe we should wait on the ring and find Adevem instead."

"Kitty says it's too late. You already blabbed about where you left Serafina."

"I didn't tell…" His voice trailed off as he realized he'd mentioned her location to Jeebrelle and Babette just moments ago. The Shaitan must have been listening somehow. "My family cave is hidden."

Meow.

"Kitty says think again."

A chilling statement. "I have to go."

Despite the humans around, he stepped behind a potted plant and through a portal, accompanied by his companions. He emerged in his family cave and, as Kitty warned, arrived too late.

Serafina was gone, and only a note remained in her place.

Your mate for the ring.

Chapter Twenty-Five

Forget falling back asleep. Israfil left, and Serafina couldn't stop thinking of him. The man, the mystery, the dragon, the magician. Every moment with him brought a new revelation. Being with him had raised her bar when it came to sex. He stimulated not just her body but also her mind. She had so many questions, starting with, what did he want from her?

He'd brought her to his childhood home. It had to mean something.

Did she want it to mean something?

The whole thing was crazy if she thought about it too hard, hence why she focused on the positive. Essentially, Israfil.

He made her feel…special. Not just in bed, either. He treated her with a sweetness that appeared reserved only for her. She could see it by the surprise in Jeebrelle's expression. Especially when he mentioned having kids with her.

Freaking kids. She'd be lying if she said she'd not thought of it. She'd hit thirty a few years ago, and it was as if she could hear the ticking of a clock.

Running out of time... If she wanted children in her life, she'd have to do something soon. But was Israfil the right man? After all, she'd have a life measurably short by his standards. Israfil was thousands of years old, making her wonder how he would age. Would this be a case of her getting old while he remained young? That would suck.

But at the same time, could she really walk away?

"Given thy mate is a mage, they expected better security."

The unexpected voice had Serafina sitting upright suddenly in the bed, the blanket clutched to her bare chest. "Who is that? Who's here?"

"Have thou forgotten them already?"

Serafina must be dreaming again, had to be, because how else would Adevem, that strange character created by her mind, with that distinctive voice, be standing in Israfil's home? Although he didn't appear as before. Despite sounding the same, he possessed a body of dark smoke that undulated and shifted, as if struggling to stay together.

"Go away." She closed her eyes and willed

herself to wake. She must have fallen back asleep when Israfil left to fetch breakfast.

The annoying man didn't depart. "They will leave once thou give them the ring."

Her eyes shot open. "I don't have the ring."

"Liar. Thou confronted the vampire. Killed her and her minions. Got past her protections. Why else but to fetch the ring?"

"We did all that, but we didn't find a ring." Mostly because they'd never even looked. Too busy having sex. And now, her subconscious nagged, making her wonder if they should have searched the quarters. How many treasures could that vampire queen have hidden? That bracelet she'd used to control Israfil might have been only the tip of that iceberg.

When Israfil returned, she'd have to talk to him about it. Return to that icky place if only to quell that curiosity. It made her wonder about the hair clip she'd grabbed. A gaudy, heavy metal thing inset with a massive opal. She'd assumed it was fake because of its size, but what if it were real? It might be worth a fortune.

"Thy mate claimed the same thing. And yet, who else would have taken it?"

"Maybe it's still there. Why don't you go look?" she sassed. Why couldn't she have a pleasant dream, one where Israfil snuggled in bed with her?

"They cannot. The underground warren is

warded against Shaitan. Thou were supposed to retrieve it for them."

"What happened to don't find the ring?" she retorted.

"They expected disobedience. Is that not a trait of humanity, to do the opposite of what they are told?" Spoken with a sneer. Not completely inaccurate.

"Well, excuse me, but we didn't find your ring, and even if we did, I wouldn't give it to you."

"Thou are impertinent."

"It's one of my more redeeming traits."

Adevem didn't agree. "Humans are a blight on this planet. One that requires pruning."

"Excuse me?"

"Thou are not excused." He stared at her unblinking, and the longer she stared back, the more inhuman he became and not just because he appeared made of dark smoke.

"What is it you really want?"

"What they have always wanted. To end the world. And to do that, they need the ring, for soon for the planets will be aligned."

"Well, too bad so sad, I don't have it. Go bother someone else. Or don't. Israfil will be back soon, and he'll wake me up and you'll go bye-bye."

The strange smoky man neared. "Thou aren't sleeping."

"You're not real." As if denying it would make it true.

"Thou art stupid, like all other humans. But they will grant thee a boon for free. They will leave, but not alone. Thou will come with them."

"I'm not going anywhere with you."

"Too late. Thou already have." Adevem bobbed his head, and the cave disappeared, as did the bed. The blankets. Everything.

She glanced around at the foggy green glass walls all around. "Where have you taken me?"

"The one place thy mate will never find. The prison he placed me in."

Chapter Twenty-Six

K itty's servant was upset. He had returned to that lovely hole in the mountain with the many nooks and crannies to find the female servant, his mate, gone.

He didn't appear happy at that situation. Neither was Kitty because, hello, they forgot to feed her breakfast. While Israfil roared and shook the mountain, Kitty perched by a brazier and cleaned her butt because it had been a few minutes since she last licked it.

As she ensured fur-tastic perfection, she listened to the unfolding drama.

"How could I be so stupid? I should have never left her." Israfil lamented and paced, the note he'd found already burned to ash.

"You couldn't know the Shaitan would go after her." Jeebrelle's soothing tone did nothing to alleviate his ire. Probably because he was to blame. Blabbing about their secret hideaway. Idiot.

"Stop freaking out, dude. She's not dead." Babette didn't tolerate his whining.

"So the bastard claims."

Which led to Babette asking, "Do genies have parents? I thought they were kind of like amoeba and just kind of split in two or more." His glare had her shrugging. "Sorry. Curious mind and all."

Kitty could understand that. She wondered about so many things. Lost a life when she decided to find out what came first, the chicken or the egg. Turned out it was the farmer with a shotgun.

"We have to find Adevem." Israfil's simple plan.

"Even if you do, then what? You don't have the ring to trade, and I doubt he will let you get close enough to kill him. And would you take that risk with Serafina in his clutches?" Jeebrelle argued.

"I can't do nothing."

"How about instead of using your kill-every-thing brain you use the one that concentrates on finding the ring," Babette suggested.

"Because I'm sure it will be simple to find," he drawled sarcastically. "If it were, Adevem would have already gotten his smoky hands on it."

"Only if it's somewhere a genie can go. What if he was prevented?" Babette pointed to Kitty. "Didn't Kitty say it was found?"

At the mention of her name, Kitty stretched. "Correct. The ring is no longer in the catacombs."

"That cat just confirmed it. The ring has been picked up by someone. We just need to find them."

"Who? How? We don't have time to be scouring the planet."

"We go back and see if we can find a scent," Babette suggested.

"Waste of time." Kitty yawned.

"Maybe Kitty knows who took it." Jeebrelle eyed her with question.

"I do."

Babette's eyes widened. "Um, Kitty says she knows where it is."

Instantly, her male servant grabbed her and held her in front of his face. "Where? Tell me."

"Meow," was what Israfil, who lacked the skill to understand the most perfect feline language, heard. He glanced at Jeebrelle.

"What did she say? Where is the ring?"

Jeebrelle bit her lip. "She refused to say. Apparently, she's miffed at you because she hasn't been fed."

"Seriously?" He glared at Kitty.

Kitty stared right back. "Tell my servant if he wants the ring, then he'd better get me some food. After all, he's supposed to be caring for my wellbeing."

Babette smirked as she translated, and he went still. Very, very still.

Then slumped. "Fuck me." He put Kitty down and portalled out of sight. He wasn't gone long. He returned with an armful of treats.

A bottle of cream. Can of sardines. Ooh, some catnip.

Kitty spent a moment rolling in the green stuff and inhaling the much-needed nutrition while he stared adoringly at her.

Only when she stretched out and sighed did he finally ask in a soft voice, "Kitty, where is the ring?"

"Hold on a second," Kitty said before getting to her feet.

Babette once more translated, and he began to lose his composure. "This is useless. We're wasting time."

Kitty began to gag and heave, her stomach knotting and clenching. Her breakfast spewed out, and her servants admired it with a gasp.

Amidst the chewed milky sardines and the hair-ball she'd been digesting, something glinted.

"What is that?" Babette pointed.

"The ring you've been looking for," Kitty declared, feeling much better now. And hungry again. She went for round two.

Israfil grimaced and plucked the ring free.

"You've had it all this time?" Jeebrelle questioned. "Why didn't you say anything?"

The cat slurped a sardine and shrugged. "No one asked."

Surely it was her imagination because there was no way her male servant said, "I'm going to throttle that cat."

More like smother her in love because now that he had the ring, he could save his female. And just in time, too. Kitty needed a proper belly rub.

Chapter Twenty-Seven

Israfil held the ring tight in his fist. He had no fucking clue what to do with it once he'd cleaned it of cat vomit.

A cat he might just skin.

And did Kitty care? Nope. She ate to fill her empty belly and went to sleep on his bed as if Serafina wasn't in grave danger. As if Israfil knew how to find Adevem to trade it for Serafina.

He didn't. Left with only Jeebrelle and Babette, he struggled to form a plan. The note that he'd burn in his ire hadn't exactly given him a time or location to make a trade.

And he would trade. Then, once Serafina was safe, he'd kill the Shaitan bastard.

"You won't be able to kill him." Maalik suddenly arrived with Daava, the portal having formed right in the middle of his cave. He really needed to do something about his security.

Azrael also popped in with his very pregnant and human wife. Too many people interrupting his plans for vengeance.

He glared at them all. "What are you doing here?"

Maalik uttered an ominous, "I had a vision."

"What he said." Azrael pointed at the dragon mage seer. "We've come to help."

As for Daava, the former Shaitan turned dragon, she grinned ferociously as she said, "I heard we might have to kill something."

The human was the only sane one. Daphne cradled her belly as she said, "Research indicates this Adevem who took your mate might very well be the Shaitan from the last amphora we've been looking for."

"How does knowing that help?" Israfil asked.

"Because it might explain why I keep seeing foggy green glass." Maalik's useless reply.

Israfil shook his head. "Actually, that doesn't explain shit." Another new favorite expression he'd learned, which didn't help with his frustration of the moment.

"Don't be so sure," Daphne argued. "Maalik has been having a vision of green glass surrounding a woman."

"Is it Serafina?" he asked hopefully.

"I think so," Maalik said.

"Think?" he practically yelled.

"Don't yell at him!" Daava growled. "Or I will twist your lips into a knot."

Maalik smirked.

Before a fight began, Jeebrelle placed a hand on Israfil's forearm. "I know you're anxious, but keep in mind Maalik hasn't met Serafina so he has no idea if he's seeing your mate."

Daphne cleared her throat. "Getting back to the green glass, according to my historical notes, the only amphora unaccounted for is made of green glass. Is it possible this Adevem is keeping your mate prisoner inside?"

"Wouldn't it have been destroyed upon their release?" All the other Shaitan had pulverized their receptacles.

"I don't know," Daphne admitted.

"Then how does that help? Knowing she might be trapped in a bottle doesn't get us any closer to finding Serafina."

"I'm sure now that you have the ring, Adevem will contact you," Jeebrelle soothed.

"You can't give him the ring," Maalik quietly asserted. "Bad things might happen if you do."

"And if I don't? What happens to Serafina?"

Maalik's lips thinned.

"That's what I thought, so don't suggest it again." Israfil wouldn't sacrifice Serafina.

"You said bad things *might* happen." Azrael pinpointed Maalik's words. "How do we avoid the bad?"

"It's not yet clear. Only that a choice will be made, one that requires selflessness."

"Meaning she's fucked." Babette's addition to the conversation.

"I'd gladly trade my life to save hers," Israfil growled.

"I'm sure you would, but what if it comes down to an entire world versus her?"

"You won't like my answer." Israfil gave up everything once upon a time for the world. This time? He'd willingly give his life, but not hers. Never her.

"All of this is moot until we find the genie," Babette pointed out. "Should we split up and search?"

Daava, who'd crouched and stared eye to eye with Kitty, snapped her fingers. "The feline claims to know where the Shaitan is located."

Israfil sighed. Not again. He turned to his cat. "Where? And don't you dare give me the runaround like you did with the artifact."

"Meow."

Daava appeared amused as she said, "She says you need to ask her nicely."

He gritted his jaw. "Please, Kitty, where can I find Adevem and Serafina?"

"Meow-meow-meow."

All the women arched their brows and then glanced at each other.

"What?" he snapped.

It was Jeebrelle who hesitatingly said, "Kitty says they're nearby, inside this mountain."

"Impossible. Do you see a Shaitan?" he snapped, sweeping a hand.

"The feline says you can get to the Shaitan via the treasure room." Daava cocked her head. "I really need one of those for my collection. Maalik?"

"Fear not, I see us building one if we survive the day."

Israfil ignored them as he thought back to what he'd seen in the room of riches. Could the missing amphora be in there? He'd not yet taken an account of everything.

With long strides, he reached the stone wall and a pass of his hands slid it open to reveal the mounds of gold and jewels, but no Shaitan. Nor a bottle.

"Tell Kitty she's full of shit," he bellowed. "There's no one in here."

"She says to watch your tone, and that is the wrong treasure room. You must first access the secret pass-through chamber your father built."

"My father never built a thing in his life."

"Apparently he did after you were caught up in the spell that bound you to the Shaitan." Daava kept translating his cat's meowed speech.

"Where?" He stomped toward Kitty. "How do I reach it?"

Kitty stretched. Meowed. Caused the women to smother laughs.

"Tell me what she said."

"She said passage to the secret treasure room can be accessed via your mother's boudoir of dicks."

He blinked. "Excuse me?"

Jeebrelle bit her lip, so Babette answered for her. "This might come as a shock, big boy, but your mom hoarded dicks. Dildos. Carved penises. According to the cat, the way to the hidden place with the Shaitan can be accessed by tugging the right dick."

"And where is this supposed room of phalluses?" It had to be a lie. As if his mother would hoard such a thing.

"Behind the shield." Daava pointed.

He didn't need to look to know the shield spoken of. It had always hung on the wall since he was a hatchling. It didn't move. He'd tried more than once to play with it.

Stomping toward it, he eyed its dull, silvery surface before grabbing it. It didn't budge. He grunted and pulled, only to have the human, her belly leading the way, shoo him aside.

"Let me try."

"Go ahead." He crossed his arms and waited.

Daphne eyed the shield then the wall, before grabbing a cold sconce and twisting it. With a grinding noise, the shield swung to the side, revealing a door.

He scowled but grunted, "Thanks."

The spell on the door had long since lost its power, so it opened easily onto a room of dicks. Everywhere he looked, phalluses of all shapes and sizes. An item no mother should ever own because mothers did not have sex.

His stomach roiled at the sight of so many of them. How could his father have let his mother hoard such a thing? Worse was the embarrassment as his companions crowded inside the room and uttered exclamations.

But when Babette said, "Hey, can I borrow this one?" he snapped.

"We're not here to play but find my mate. Where is the lever to open the entrance for the secret treasure room?"

No one answered. They didn't have to, as their gazes all went to the pedestal with its very detailed phallus labeled: Husband.

Israfil closed his eyes and cringed as he pulled on the dick.

Click.

The floor behind the pedestal shifted, and he saw stairs going down.

Before he could lead the charge, Kitty did.

Sigh.

Forget emasculation. He'd been cat-asculated.

Chapter Twenty-Eight

As a child, Serafina had watched an old show called *I Dream of Jeannie*. A fun sitcom with a loveable genie who'd been freed from a bottle. A bottle that proved luxurious inside with cushions and sumptuous fabrics.

The reality? Quite different. The bottle she'd been trapped in didn't have a comfy couch. It lacked furniture of any kind, along with windows and food. Not even a pot to piss in, which might end up a problem if she stayed in here too long.

Already, she had no idea of how much time passed, only that it felt like an eternity. She pounded on the glass and shouted herself hoarse. How long would she be trapped in here? How long before she went completely insane?

Only when she slumped in despair did Adevem return.

The genie had released his grip the bottom half of his form and looked more as expected with a smoky tail. "There's no point in trying to escape. Especially given thy lack of magic. They would know. Three thousand years they spent inside this prison."

While she hated to encourage him, she found herself asking, "How did you escape?"

"Not easily. It took so long to chisel at the stopper. Three thousand years. But eventually freedom was achieved."

"You must have been so relieved."

"They were overjoyed only until they realized the limitations of their freedom."

"Is that why you want to find this ring? So you can release your friend?"

"Friend?" He looked as if he sucked on a lemon, his distaste so great. "They have no friends, only purpose. A purpose they thought impossible once a few were lost and the rest wanted to abandon the plan. They showed them the error of their way."

Something ominous in those words had her frowning. "I don't understand."

"Because thou are a simple-minded flesh bag. Thou cannot grasp the greatness they are capable of, and neither could they. Hence why they had to be consumed for the greater good."

"Wait, what do you mean by consumed?"

For a moment, Adevem stared at her with his

usual expression, and then his head bulged and stretched into a few distinct faces, all of them open mouthed as if screaming. A blink of her eyes and it went back to one placid expression.

Horror filled her. "You ate the other genies?"

"They are now stronger as a single entity. And when the planets align, with the addition of the one bound inside the ring, they will finally achieve that which has been in the making since their arrival."

That really didn't sound good. "Achieve what, exactly?"

"They have realized that the Iblis isn't needed for domination, for they shall become greater once the door opens to their previous dimension and they consume enough to be unstoppable."

"You want to become a mega genie?" Her eyebrows practically jumped off her forehead. "It won't happen. Israfil will never allow it."

"He will if he wishes to have thee returned."

"He's not going to trade me for the world." As romantic as it might sound. A man who'd voluntarily imprisoned himself for thousands of years wouldn't sacrifice all he'd done for her.

Could smoke rub its hand in proper glee? This one did. "A mate will do anything for love. Even as they speak, Israfil and his companions draw near, marching to their deaths. There is irony in the fact the dragon mages fought for nothing for, in the end, they shall win."

"You're not going to win. Israfil will stop you."
Sure, it might be pointless arguing with this alien
megalomaniac, but she did it nonetheless.

"They can't be beaten. Even without the ring,
they are too strong." His head lifted, and he smiled,
wider than was humanly possible with shadowy
shark-like teeth.

"Israfil will find a way."

"Thy hope is misplaced." The genie cocked its
head. "They arrive."

Poof.

The genie disappeared, leaving her stuck in a
bottle. The thick glass muffled sight and sound,
despite that she could hear the murmur of voices
then a shout.

Israfil! He'd come, and had no idea of the
danger. She had to warn him, but how?

Chapter Twenty-Nine

The stairs went down and around for miles, or so Babette complained. "This isn't natural. Dragons are supposed to fly, not burrow underground like moles."

Israfil agreed despite the fact he'd now spent most of his life in caves. On the other hand, caves and tight spaces didn't bother him. Jeebrelle, however, showed signs of anxiety.

Babette wrapped an arm around her. "It's okay, Jeebs. Breathe. You're okay. You're not back in that prison."

A soft reminder that tightened Maalik's expression. After all, he was the reason they'd not seen the light of day for three thousand years. And yet, if they'd not sacrificed, they wouldn't be here now to fight the Shaitan, and Israfil wouldn't have met Serafina.

"Does anyone have a plan once we find Adevem?" he asked.

"Poke him with the pointy end of your stick?" Babette suggested.

"I'm thinking that by the look on Maalik's face it might not be that easy," Jeebrelle mumbled.

The man appeared confused. "There's a darkness in the future that I can't discern. Beyond it, only two paths emerge."

"Let me guess, one of them is death," Azrael grumbled. He'd been scowling since they'd begun their descent. He'd had his pregnant mate transferred to the care of the Silvergrace family while he went to save the world.

Jeebrelle had tried to convince Babette to stay with Daphne—*"This is a fight that will be won with magic. You'll be safer if you stay behind."* To which Babette had replied, *"Suck my clit. You ain't leaving me here to miss all the fun."*

So here they were, four dragon mages from a time long ago, one silver dragon with too much courage, and a former Shaitan determined to preserve the life she'd chosen.

Would it be enough?

Azrael let him keep the God Killer, and for that Israfil was thankful even as Maalik's lips pinched. He was hiding something, but at least he was smart enough to keep quiet about it.

The ring Israfil clutched in his free hand,

unwilling to let it go until he had to. He could feel the pulse of the Shaitan within, hear its voice whispering, not for freedom. It begged him to kill it now because it feared a fate worse than death.

What did Adevem have planned? For he had no doubt the Shaitan had a devious plot. It still stunned him to realize his father had chosen to hide one of the artifacts. Obviously not well enough since Adevem was found. How odd, though, that he'd returned to the place of his prison.

The stairs ended abruptly at a door, wide open in welcome. Everyone tensed in preparation. No shifting, though. The lack of space meant they had to keep their two-legged shapes, putting them at a distinct disadvantage.

"I'll go first." Stave in hand, ring in the other, Israfil entered.

Past the threshold, they found themselves in a massive cavern with a river running through it. Too wide to be leaped across. The current brisk enough that it would require a strong swimmer. In the middle of that flow, a jutting island of rock, flat but for the pedestal in the center of it and leaning against it, Adevem. Alone.

Israfil strode to the very edge of the water. "Where's Serafina?"

"Where's the ring?" In this deep place, the Shaitan wore its smoky body rather than a human.

Israfil held out his hand to show it. "I've done my part. Where is she?"

"Somewhere safe. Unlike you." The Shaitan smirked, and he flowed from the rocky island to float above the water, only his upper half retaining any kind of shape.

"The deal was the ring for Serafina."

"As if you planned to honor it."

"What would you know of honor, Shaitan!" Azrael was the first to lunge to attack. The change into his dragon shape began but never finished, as something with a metallic clang shot from the water.

Azrael cried out as a collar wrapped around his neck and sealed shut, quelling his dragon and dropping him to his knees.

"Dracinore," Jeebrelle murmured. The one thing that made them weak.

"Double-crossing bastard!" Israfil ran for the Shaitan, but rather than shift, he hefted the spear, pulled his arm back to throw. It never went forward. A manacle shot from the flowing water and grabbed his wrist. The slack in the chain tightened and dragged him to the ground.

He could only turn his head to avoid smashing his face, meaning he saw Maalik similarly tethered. Beyond the seer, Daava hissed and managed to shift into her unique dragon shape with a single horn projecting from her forehead.

A net of finely woven dracinore dropped from the ceiling and covered her, smothering her body but not her scream of pain and rage.

Maalik thrashed. "Daava!"

"You fucking asshole." Babette cursed as she bolted past Israfil, snaring the stave on her way.

The woman managed to leap and throw. A good toss that the Shaitan avoided with a smirk. Their only real weapon soared harmlessly past and landed in the river.

Gone.

The distraction allowed Jeebrelle to shift and blow her poisonous gas next. To no avail. The Shaitan never did react to normal threats.

More shackles emerged from the water, binding Jeebrelle, leading Babette to cry out, "Jeebs, don't worry, I'll save you."

Not true. Adevem had prepared more than enough manacles. She could do nothing.

None of them could. The dracinore chains removed their ability to shift. Sapped their strength and will.

Only then did Adevem come close, moving on a tail of smoke. The Shaitan hovered in front of Israfil and held out a smoky hand.

"Hand over the ring."

"No." Even he understood now just how gravely they'd miscalculated. Adevem had obviously somehow seen this moment and prepared. Israfil, in his desperation to save his mate, had walked into a trap.

"Thou have lost, Israfil. Thou cannot stop what happens next." Adevem reached with a smoky hand, and Israfil gasped at the pain in his fingers. They spasmed, releasing the ring.

It rose, buoyed by magic, right into Adevem's grip. The Shaitan smirked. "At last." He squeezed it. What emerged from the broken metal had no real shape but a loud voice that screamed as Adevem absorbed the spirit released from the ring.

"Oh, that's not good," Maalik muttered. "We weren't supposed to let that happen."

"And you couldn't mention this before?" Israfil snapped.

"I told you I couldn't see this part of the battle."

"So what are we to do now?" he growled.

"Now, thou all will die." Adevem's hand turned into a scything blade. "Did thou know that they also had a seer? They foresaw they would fail in the past, and thus they prepared for the future. They bided their time for more than three thousand years. Waiting. Knowing this moment would come. And now all they need is the lifeblood of five mages. The question being, which of thee shall die first? Not thee, Israfil, for thou shall have the honor of watching all thy companions die."

"So this is about revenge?" Israfil snapped.

"As if they are ruled by such petty emotion.

This is about ultimate power and an end to flesh and the beginning of them. Thou are the key that will open the door."

"A door to where?" Babette asked.

It was Daava, grim faced and despairing, who said, "To where we came from."

And if that happened, this world as they knew it would die.

Chapter Thirty

All of Kitty's servants had been captured. How annoying. All but one and Kitty could hear her yelling inside the bottle forgotten atop the pedestal. To reach it, she'd have to cross a river.

Kitty hated water. However, she hated the idea of the entire world dying even more. After all, who would serve or feed her if everyone was dead? The thought of no more belly rubs, warm cream, or someone to carry her had Kitty girding herself.

While the smoky irritant that captured her servants boasted of their intelligence, she eyed the problem at hand. Fast-moving water. Too quick to swim. The calculation of angle and speed had her heading to the mouth of the river and jumping in there.

The water proved as gross as expected. Cold. Wet. Kitty hated it, and yet she paddled hard to angle herself to hit that island of rock. Shivering and annoyed at the things a goddess had to do, she climbed up and then up again to the top of the pedestal, where a small green glass bottle rested.

Now what? She could hear her servant inside the bottle. How to get her out? A cat did what she knew best and knocked it off the shelf.

Crash.

The glass shattered, and there was a yell, a few of them actually. The most strident being the smoky man, who exclaimed, "What have you done?"

Solved a few problems. For one, despite the Shaitan's ability to move around and meddle, he'd still been tethered to his prison so when Kitty fully freed Adevem from his bottle, she earned three wishes. The second benefit? From the shattered remains a bilious smoke billowed, and inside that smog...

"Serafina." Israfil shouted her name as the woman coughed and choked.

The Shaitan, whose prison Kitty had broken, began moving toward her with ominous intent.

The first fireball singed a whisker.

"My whisker!" Kitty screeched. "I'm hideous."

"Do something," Serafina hissed as she clutched Kitty and tucked behind the pedestal. A better spot than in the open where fireballs and lightning bolts caused much damage.

"Must I do everything?" Kitty complained.

After all, she'd found the ring, led them here, and now they wanted to be saved. A goddess's work was never done.

Very well.

Kitty shoved out of the snuggly embrace, pounced into the open, and got hit by lightning.

Died. Lost a life, immediately returned, and yowled, only to almost die again as a rock fell from the ceiling.

A good thing she wished it to land elsewhere. How unfortunate it landed on the seer's head and knocked him out. Guess he didn't see that coming.

Oops, on using a wish though. Now she only had two wishes left. Her tiny brain spun with plans, only to have them all shredded as a dark rope of fog wrapped around Serafina's neck and dragged her into the open.

"Let go of my servant at once!" Kitty yodeled.

"Is that a wish?" the Shaitan sneered. "Go ahead and waste it."

He'd like that. Being ornery, Kitty opted to do something unexpected. Rather than wishing to free Serafina, she wished for Serafina to have the ability to free herself.

Had Adevem been a regular Shaitan, the request might have chosen the path of least resistance. Like giving Serafina the strength to break free. However, Adevem had been absorbing all the other genies he'd found. It made him stronger.

Hence the wish provided more than bargained for.

Serafina gasped, and her body arched. For a moment, it appeared as if nothing happened, and then Serafina's hands began to glow as she grabbed the smoke choking her.

The Shaitan screamed in actual pain and released her. Serafina rose to her feet and stared at her hands. Then her gaze narrowed as she eyed the floating genie. The first fireball she lobbed wobbled and missed, splashing uselessly against the far cavern wall.

The next seared past the Shaitan's tail, and he hissed, "Thou shall pay for that!"

"How about you pay first for stuffing me in that jar, asshole?"

The pair began lobbing insults and magic, the fireworks quite interesting and the outcome undetermined until the Shaitan realized he wasted time —and might just lose.

Adevem did the one thing guaranteed to stop Serafina in her tracks. He turned his smoky hand into a sword and held it to Israfil's neck. "Attack and he dies."

Serafina's hands lowered even as Israfil growled, "Kill the Shaitan."

"I can't." Her female servant's lower lip trembled.

Damned emotional two-legged beings.

"Move aside, servant." Kitty strode past, her tail high, to confront the arrogant Shaitan.

"Go ahead, you mangy feline. Use your last wish," the bad genie said. "Beg me to save his life. Because the moment you do, I'll be free. And you'll all die."

She had no doubt he would murder them all, and while she still had a few lives, she was rather fond of her first male servant.

Kitty had only one wish left. She could have demanded a never-ending supply of sardines. A dish of cream that remained full and warm. The adulation of all humankind.

Instead, she did something very unlike her. She thought of others.

I wish...

Chapter Thirty-One

Israfil blinked. Then closed his eyes for a long moment before opening them again.

But the Shaitan had disappeared.

"Where did it go?"

It was Serafina, eyeing hands that a second ago had been lobbing fireballs, who translated his cat's meow. "Kitty says she wished the Shaitan would go back where they came from."

"Er, what?" Israfil must have misunderstood.

Only Maalik, sitting up and rubbing his head, confirmed it. "They're gone."

"It can't be that simple," Israfil exclaimed as he sat up, grimacing as the metal collar clanked with each movement.

It was Daava who had the answer. "I think that the wish was only possible because the dimension the Shaitan originally came from was close."

"So they're gone? For good?" Jeebrelle exclaimed.

"Meow-da-meow."

"For those who didn't understand, Kitty says yes and you're welcome. She also wants to know who wants the honor of carrying her over the river." Serafina bit her lower lip as she eyed the torrent. "I could use a hand, too."

They all could, only the dracinore chains remained in place, rendering them all useless, which was when Luc arrived stomping and grumbling, "Before you ask, Elspeth sent me. No, I'm not happy about it given she's in labor, but she says she's not pushing until I free your annoying asses." The demon, in his man shape but wearing horns, went to everyone and easily freed them. Once he did, Israfil could change into his dragon and create a bridge for his mate.

Kitty crossed first. Serafina appeared hesitant but went across, too. Once she was safe, he shifted back and hugged her and whispered, "I love you."

And to his eternal pleasure, she whispered back, "I love you, too."

They weren't the only ones professing their affection. Daava soothed Maalik, Luc became Kitty's newest disciple by scratching her above the tail, and Babette, who'd grabbed the twisted and broken ring, got down on one knee in front of Jeebrelle.

Silence fell as the silver dragon proposed. "Jeebs, you are the only woman for me. I know you're my mate and all, but I love you and would be honored if you became my wife."

Jeebrelle cried and nodded. And things might have gotten sappier if Luc didn't snap, "Can we leave now? My wife needs to give birth."

Since they knew where they were going, a portal was called, and everyone went through it except for Kitty, Israfil, and Serafina.

Despite her protests, he carried her all the way up those stairs. Kitty, too.

Unfortunately, his plans to make love to his mate were curtailed by a yowling cat.

He sighed. "I know, she's hungry."

And Kitty had earned it. By using her wishes to save them all rather than filling her belly, she'd shown a selflessness that deserved a reward.

A portal brought him to a store where he could exchange a tiara for money. With the money, he bought so much food Kitty passed out with a rounded belly. There was even enough left over to handle her if she woke up needing a snack.

Only then was he finally able to strip Serafina and bathe her with his hands, stroking every inch of her body. Then he made love to her until she gasped and cried out his name. The pain as she zapped him with her new magic didn't detract from his pleasure at all.

He went to sleep that night knowing for the first time in forever he had a future and a reason to look forward to tomorrow.

Epilogue

Serafina's life changed overnight, and not just because a dragon mage claimed her as his mate and she'd been a part of saving the world. Being a sorceress had its challenges, such as accidentally zapping her lover during sex. He claimed it added an element of danger that only made her sexier, but she worried about accidentally killing him or someone else. Hence why they'd been having lessons that usually ended in her getting annoyed, blowing up some rocks, and him seducing her.

Not exactly the worst thing that could have happened.

The genie threat had been eradicated and by a cat who smugly lorded it over everyone for being the most brilliant mind ever known. Kitty had a point. Sometimes the simplest solutions worked best.

Speaking of simple, Serafina smoothed her new gown down over her hips. It was a straight design with no ruffles or bling despite the suggestions to add some. She eyed her flat belly. Not for long. The doctor—who Babette called Aunt Yolanda—had confirmed it. She had a baby in there. Human or dragon or something else? No one could say quite yet, but daddy was over the moon.

Also, super protective. "Are you sure you should be wearing those?" Israfil pointed to her heels. "What if you trip in them and fall?"

"I expect you to catch me if that happens."

"Good point," he agreed. "As if I'd ever let you fall."

"You look dashing." She smiled as she eyed him in his suit.

He tugged at the collar. "It's uncomfortable."

"Too bad. I like it, and after all, we are expected to dress nice since it is a wedding."

A wedding long anticipated, as Babette and Jeebrelle were tying the knot and everyone was attending. Even Elspeth and her new baby, with a father who scowled at everyone but beamed at his wife and child.

The brides both wore dresses, Babette in flowing white, contrasting with the wild red curls of her hair, which matched her lipstick. Jeebrelle chose a frothy concoction of pale yellow, her long hair bound in intricate loops pinned with the opal clip that once belonged to a vampire queen. Something old and borrowed. Her garter, which made her blush when it was explained how it would be removed, being the something new.

The golden dragon king presided over the ceremony looking properly regal. Many people cried.

Even Kitty sniffled and said, "I suppose I'll have to release them from service for the honeymoon. They'd better bring me back a treat from the islands."

The pair were vacationing in Hawaii.

Israfil turned out to be quite the dancer once challenged by Maalik. He spun and dipped Serafina until she was breathless, and then he kissed her until she whispered, "Can we go home?"

That night in bed in their mountain home, she laid her head on Israfil's chest and whispered, "I am so glad we found each other."

"It was fate," he declared.

To which Kitty snorted. "You're welcome." A reminder that, for them, there would never be a dull moment.

KITTY LEFT the lovers to their disgusting smooching. The whole licking each other's mouths was gross.

Why couldn't they just stick to the bum? That at least she understood.

With only three of her lives left—having lost one just recently when she chased that squirrel up the pole and got electrocuted—she had decided to be more careful; however, that didn't cure her curious nature.

Tail high, she wandered down to the cavern with its pedestal and noticed the river had dropped enough to show off some stepping stones that allowed her to cross while keeping her paws dry. On the other side, an intriguing crack beckoned. She followed it, past the glowing lichen, chasing some skittish rats then being hunted by a spider that apparently thought she was dinner. Almost lost a life there until something bigger ate it.

Eventually she emerged into a cave warmed by a lava waterfall. Within that space, Kitty found an old woman weaving at a loom, her fingers flying as she fed it many different colored threads. She squinted at Kitty and shook her head.

"You shouldn't be here. You're an anomaly in the pattern."

"Is that so?" drawled Kitty. She sauntered closer for a peek at what the woman wrought. So many bright hues and patterns. She reached out a paw to touch.

"Don't you dare." The woman shook her finger.

Kitty cocked her head. Had that woman just ordered a goddess?

That old woman followed up her threat with a squirt from a spray bottle, chastising Kitty with a warning. "Stay away from the threads of time."

"I will if you feed me," Kitty demanded, choosing to curl up in a basket of cast-off spools that formed a lumpy bed.

"I'll make us both something warm to eat. Don't move."

Kitty might have listened if a dangling thread from the loom didn't taunt her. It hung there, wiggling faintly, a rebel in obvious need of correction. She pounced on that evil strand and pulled it free of the tapestry.

Which was how she accidentally started the end of the world for the second time.

Have we seen the last of the dragons and Kitty? Probably not. So stayed tuned. In the meantime, sink your teeth into more shapeshifters with Growl and Prowl or find some more amazing stories at EveLanglais.com